Shayna Gunther—
Ms. Efficiency herself—
puts together a list of the most eligible bachelors around

1. The Computer Guy. Smart, hardworking, a successful businessman. Unfortunately, he's already in love—with *himself*. Too bad he isn't sweet and caring like, say, Max Winston. (But then, Max isn't even *on* her list....)

2. Mr. Six-Hundred-Dollar Suit. *Very* well dressed. Which explains why he got downright nasty when she accidentally dumped an entire strawberry cheesecake on him. Now, *Max* would just have laughed and helped her clean up the mess. (But maybe Shayna should try to remember that Max is absolutely *not* on her list....)

3. The Nightclub Owner. Sophisticated, charming, absolutely nothing wrong with him. (Except that he's simply not Max "Not-Even-on-the-Gosh-Darn-List" Winston...)

Dear Reader,

Chain letters! Don't you just hate them? Thanks to the joys of E-mail (and most of the time it really *is* a joy), I seem to receive them on pretty much a daily basis. The worst thing is, I keep getting the same ones over and over. No, I take that back. The worst thing really is that none of them ever come true. I'm still making ends meet but not getting rich, and I certainly haven't met Mr. Right. Luckily for Shayna Gunther, heroine of Robyn Amos's debut Yours Truly novel, *Bachelorette Blues,* her chain-letter experience has a happier outcome. She *does* meet her perfect match—though it takes her a little while to figure that out. (Just for the record: *I* would have recognized him a *lot* sooner!)

After you finish enjoying Shayna and Max's story, move on to the final installment of Karen Templeton's fabulous WEDDINGS, INC. trilogy. *Wedding? Impossible!* turns out not to be so impossible after all, of course. Admittedly, Zoe's a bit wary of her supposedly perfect blind date, Mike, but who wouldn't be? (If you say you wouldn't, you've never been on a blind-date disaster!) But pretty soon she's hooked, agreeing with everyone else's opinion of Mike—that he's wonderful—and planning that extremely possible wedding after all.

Enjoy! And remember to come back next month for two more books all about the fun of meeting—and marrying!—Mr. Right.

Yours,

Leslie J. Wainger
Executive Senior Editor

Please address questions and book requests to:
Silhouette Reader Service
U.S.: 3010 Walden Ave., P.O. Box 1325, Buffalo, NY 14269
Canadian: P.O. Box 609, Fort Erie, Ont. L2A 5X3

ROBYN AMOS

Bachelorette Blues

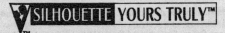

Published by Silhouette Books
America's Publisher of Contemporary Romance

This book is dedicated to my local RWA chapter,
Washington Romance Writers. Their members have
proven that, with solidarity, endurance and support,
even the worst of luck is only temporary.

 SILHOUETTE BOOKS

ISBN 0-373-52086-7

BACHELORETTE BLUES

Copyright © 1999 by Robyn Amos

Printed in U.S.A.

Letter from Robyn Amos

Is it luck or coincidence? You tell me. One week after I came up with the chain letter idea for *Bachelorette Blues*, I received a chain letter of my own in the mail. Thanks to the immediacy of E-mail, I received countless chain letters while writing this novel. Some promised true love, like the one Shayna receives from her niece; others promised good fortune or wealth. All I know is, I haven't participated in any of them, and my luck has never been better. Of course, I'm still working on the true love and the wealth.

I'm not superstitious…much. I'm a firm believer that if you don't *finish* reading the chain letter, it doesn't count. Fortunately, I've never been as clumsy as Shayna, but I wouldn't mind having her organizational skills to help me balance my full-time job, writing career, friends and family. Maybe I like the concept of Shayna being a life management consultant so much because I need one so desperately.

Besides collecting chain letters, while writing this book I went duckpin bowling for the first time, picked up a few new recipes—now I just have to learn to like cooking—and paid homage to my love of chocolate. If you like Shayna and Max's story, or just want to send me a chain letter—I'm just kidding; no chain letters, please!—contact me at: P.O. Box 7904, Gaithersburg, MD 20898-7904.

Robyn Amos

1

Curiosity nagged at Shayna Gunther like the box of chocolate cookies stashed in her desk drawer. She plucked the envelope out of her In bin and studied it. Rain had smeared the blue ink, blurring the return address.

With a jewel-handled letter opener, Shayna sliced through the envelope and pulled out a wrinkled, wide-ruled sheet of notebook paper.

Just her luck. Her nine-year-old niece, Tiffany, had sent her a chain letter. Shaking her head in amusement, Shayna read the childish scrawl.

This is not a joke or a prank. It is very serious. If you follow these instructions carefully, you will find true love. Within seventy-two hours, you must copy this letter six times and mail it to six friends who are looking for love. At midnight, on the third day, drink a glass of water and say the name of a boy or girl you like. He or she will be yours forever. If you break the chain, beware. Bad luck will be yours. Forever.

With a sound somewhere between a laugh and a sigh, Shayna picked up the phone on her desk. She normally called her sister Nicole on Sunday afternoons, but this just couldn't wait.

"Hi Nic, it's Shayna."

"Shayna? What's wrong? Are you switching from Sundays to Wednesdays?"

"Come on, I'm not *that* bad." Shayna was used to being teased about her predictability, but she didn't let it get to her. The talent for organization was her unique gift.

"Girl, I knew you were *'that'* bad when you started color coding your underwear with the days of the week. Yellow on Sundays, pink on Mondays…"

"Nicole, stop. I was only eight. That was just a phase." She still wore blue on Tuesdays, but Nicole didn't have to know that.

"Yeah, a phase. That's why you make your living creating schedules and routines for other people to follow."

"I make good money as a life management consultant, and you know it."

Knowing what Shayna was like in high school, Nicole, of all people, should understand. Shayna had never had her sister's easy popularity and self-confidence. For years, if anyone was tripping over bleachers at football games or spilling drinks at parties, her name was Shayna. Carefully planning for every possibility had helped her pull herself together.

"Anyway, I called about Tiffany," Shayna said, pushing old memories aside.

"Uh-oh." Nicole's voice took on a resigned what-has-my-child-done-now? tone.

"No, no. It's nothing bad. I just wanted to tell you about the letter I got from her today."

"Tif sent you a letter?"

"A *chain* letter."

Nicole's hearty laugh cut through the miles that separated Delaware from Maryland. "That's my girl. Do you want to talk to the little troublemaker?"

"Please."

"Hi, Aunt Shay," Tiffany said with a burst of excitement. Shayna could picture the girl's bright smile curving her caramel-colored cheeks.

"Hi, Tif. I got your chain letter today."

"Well." Tiffany sighed dramatically the way only nine-year-olds could. "You'd better get started right away, Aunt Shay. Mom says you're long overdue for a boyfriend."

Shayna made a mental note to strangle her sister.

"That's why I called, Tiffany. Chain letters and other superstitions don't really work. If you want something in life, you have to get it for yourself by working hard."

"Oh, but it does work. Last week, Ricky Jacobs invited me to a pizza party. Then I started liking Jimmy Hunter..."

As Tiffany continued, Shayna couldn't help noticing that a fourth grader had a more interesting social life than she did.

"Anyway, Amy Morton broke the chain, and boy, did *she* have it rough."

"What do you mean?" Shayna asked despite herself.

"First she got a D on her math test, then her parents stopped letting her watch 'Melrose Place' and then—"

"Tiffany, those were just coincidences."

"No. Her bad luck didn't go away until— What? Okay, Mom. Mom says it's time for dinner. I gotta go."

"I'll talk to you on Sunday, Tif. We can make plans for our slumber party."

"Aunt Shay? Please don't break the chain. I want you to find true love, not bad luck."

Shayna smiled. "Thanks, Tif." She hung up the phone, shaking her head. Apparently everyone knew she needed a man. She was nearing thirty, and according to her life plan it was time. But thank goodness she knew the *proper* way to go about finding the right man. Not chain letters. Not crystal balls or tarot cards. Just careful planning, plain and simple.

Shayna looked at her calendar. Each important date was color coded by event. Blue for business appointments, green for social events like movies or dinner, and purple for special occasions. She reserved red for dates with that special someone.

Unfortunately her calendar hadn't seen red ink for months. There hadn't been room in her schedule for dating. But that was about to change.

Shayna touched the purple lettering written in the block for next Saturday. "MBO Cocktail Mixer." The local chapter of the Minority Business Owners, a support group for the self-employed, had been her salvation for the past three years. Now that her consulting business was taking off, the organization was going to help her find the perfect man.

Through careful research, Shayna had compiled a list of the MBO's most eligible bachelors. They were all successful enough to be her equal, intelligent enough to bring good genes to the union and handsome enough to give her goose bumps. Any of the three men would be a good catch, but Phillip Browning, Jr., the owner of SoftTech Computer Consulting, headed the list. He dressed impeccably, spoke articulately and still had all his hair.

Shayna casually tossed the chain letter into her recycling bin as she reviewed her well-laid plans for Saturday evening. Yes, Phillip Browning, Jr. had definite potential, and in just four short days, she would know if he was "the one."

Max Winston turned onto Wisconsin Avenue and headed for the Chevy Chase Holiday Inn. His windshield wipers were keeping perfect time with the old Motown song playing on the radio. The digital clock on his dashboard read 7:45. He was fifteen minutes late. Normally he didn't worry about things like that, but he knew Shayna would be one of the first to arrive. In the six months he'd been a member of MBO, he'd learned that he could set his watch by that woman. She was so organized, he'd bet she color coded her underwear by the days of the week. Black on Mondays, red on Tuesdays…

Uh-oh! Max stepped on the gas pedal, trying to make the yellow light up ahead. It wasn't wise to think about Shayna Gunther's underwear while driving.

As he sped through the intersection, he heard a wild shriek. Glancing in his rearview mirror, he saw a bag lady wrapped in a garbage bag. She was bent over, trying to hold a sheet of newspaper over her head while struggling with an umbrella the wind had turned inside out. Max grimaced. Apparently he'd sloshed her good when he'd driven through a mud puddle.

"Sorry!" he called, tooting his horn, knowing she couldn't hear him.

Twenty minutes later, Max swirled his cocktail and scanned the lounge again. Still no sign of Shayna. She was the only reason he'd bothered showing up in the first place. Now she was nowhere to be found, and he was stuck listening to the most boring guy in the room—Phillip Browning, Jr.

What was with this guy? Didn't he know that no one cared how many copies of some duller-than-dirt accounting program he'd sold this week? Of course he didn't know. He was too busy impressing *himself.*

Max surveyed the room again, this time searching for a way to exit the conversation. Hot damn. Both his prayers were answered at once. There was Shayna. Finally.

Max blinked. That *was* Shayna, wasn't it? The woman slinking into the ladies' room with her handbag covering her face had Shayna's smooth honey brown complexion and slim sexy figure, but she looked like a drowned rat. A beautiful rat, but drowned nonetheless.

It had been raining when he arrived, but not hard enough to soak her like *that*. The front of her hair was plastered to her forehead and the back had frizzed into a puffy cloud. She hobbled on one foot because she'd apparently lost the heel of her other shoe.

Max turned back to Phillip, who was so absorbed in a monologue on his new line of Microsoft knock-offs, he hadn't even noticed that Max wasn't paying attention.

"I hate to cut you off, Phil, but I see a friend I need to talk to."

Phillip's face went blank for a moment, almost as if he were startled by the sound of someone else's voice. "Sure, Matt, we'll continue this later. I want to tell you about my new antivirus product...."

Max backed away as Phillip picked up the conversation with his next victim.

Shayna stared at her reflection in the ladies' room mirror, feeling close to tears. She was a wreck. She made her living planning, preparing for the unexpected and showing others how to do the same. How could this have happened?

She leaned her forehead on the cool glass of the mirror. Her perfect evening was over before it had even gotten started. Things couldn't possibly get any worse.

"You okay in there?"

She looked up to find Max Winston peeking around the side of the ladies' room door.

"Oh my God." She tried to rake her fingers through her hair, but they got stuck in the frizzy mass. "Max, this is the ladies' room. What are you doing in here?"

He stepped through the door and leaned against it. "I was worried about you. I saw you come in, but you never came back out."

"So you decided to *join* me in the ladies' room?"

He slipped his hands into his pockets, looking quite at home. "Nobody has come in here for at least five minutes. I knew you were alone. Besides, this is just the make-up-your-face area. I still have one more door to go through before I reach the point of no return."

Shayna turned back to the mirror. Big mistake. For a split second she'd actually forgotten what a mess she was. She looked past her freestanding hair to the man behind her. Why, when she looked the worst she'd ever looked in her life, did Max Winston have to look the best she'd ever seen him?

This man, who came to every MBO meeting in T-shirts and blue jeans, was actually wearing a jacket. Pale gray. He was still wearing jeans but they were black—somehow it made a difference—and his off-white shirt had a banded collar. He looked great.

He always looked great. In fact, he would have been at the top of her list of potential suitors if it weren't for his fly-by-the-seat-of-his-pants, spontaneous attitude that went against every principle she'd built her life upon. And now he had a front-row seat to the most humiliating night of her life.

Shayna felt like crying.

Max crossed to the mirror and looked over her shoulder. "So what happened, Shayna?" He pointed to her ruined shoes. "This is a risky fashion statement even for you."

He was making jokes. Twenty-eight years of perfect grooming now amounted to no more than a silly joke. She met his eyes in the mirror. "You…want to know…what happened to me?" she asked quietly.

"Yeah, I'd like to know."

She rounded on him. "*You* want to *know* what happened to me?"

He took a step back. "I… Well… You don't have—"

"I'll tell you…what happened…to *me*." She turned back to the mirror, staring at her miserable reflection. Her voice sounded eerily calm to her own ears. "I bought a new dress just for tonight." She smoothed her hands over her expensive white sheath, as she turned to face him. "Do you like this dress?"

He nodded obediently.

"And my hair…" She reached up to touch the flyaway strands, barely aware that Max's gaze was still locked on the damp silk that clung to her curves. "I spent exactly twenty-three minutes trying to get my hair to curl like Naomi Campbell's on the cover of *Vogue*.

"I looked good." She stared at him. "I really did. When I left the house, I was feeling so good, a little rain couldn't even get me down—after all, I always carry my trusty purse-size umbrella, right?'' She laughed, almost hysterically. ''I didn't even blink when 'a little rain' turned into a full-fledged thunderstorm the moment I got out of the car to change my flat tire.''

''Ooh, that's rough,'' Max said sympathetically.

''No. It was okay. I was cool…until I discovered that my spare was flat, too.''

She held up a hand as if taking an oath. ''But, like I tell my clients, 'You *must* have a backup plan—always.' So I called AAA and my neighbor Kitty, so she could meet Mr. Tow Truck Man and tell him where to tow my car. That way, I could just hop on the bus and make it here with time to spare, right?''

''Let me guess,'' Max said, shaking his head. ''It didn't work out.''

''No! For some reason, today of all days, the bus comes five minutes early. So I'm running to catch it, and the heel on one of my two-hundred-dollar Italian shoes breaks off in a crack in the pavement. And, of course, I miss the bus.''

Max winced. ''Okay, I get the picture.''

''Wait. There's more. The next bus drops me off a block away from the hotel. So I'm walking, and the wind turns my cute little purse-size umbrella into a useless piece of junk. And there I am, in the middle of a storm. I've got a newspaper over my head to protect this glamorous hairstyle. I'm struggling with my crappy umbrella, and some jerk comes flying down the street and splatters the back of my dress with mud. Can you believe that?''

"Uh, is that your garbage bag?" he asked, pointing toward the crumpled black plastic on the counter.

"That's not a garbage bag. It's my handy-dandy-fold-up rain slicker," she said with exaggerated cheerfulness. "What's wrong? You look sick."

"I feel *really* bad—for *you*—because you've been through so much tonight."

"Don't worry about it." Shayna sighed, resigned to her fate. "It's not your fault."

Despite her reassurance, Max looked even more distressed.

"But could you do me a favor and call me a cab? I can't go out there."

Max frowned. "What? Leaving so soon? Come on now. You obviously went through a lot to get here. This evening is still salvageable."

Shayna placed a hand on her hip. "Are you kidding me? I realize that nothing in life ever fazes you, Max, but even you've got to see that I have a problem here. My dress is ruined, so are my shoes. And I don't even want to talk about my hair."

Max stepped back for a moment, studying her. "We can work with this."

Shayna just stared at him. This was a nightmare and she was going to wake up any minute.

"Let's start with the dress," he said, taking off his jacket. He handed it to her. "Try this on."

Too confused to do anything else, she put on the lightweight jacket. Of course it was too big.

Max stepped forward, rolled up the sleeves and arranged the lapels. He stepped back, surveying his work. Shayna just stood there like a dressmaker's dummy.

"Not bad." He nodded.

She turned to the full-length mirror on her right. She never would have believed it, but the jacket helped a lot. She made a full circle. The jacket just brushed the hem of her dress, hiding the mud on the back of her skirt. From the front, her dress, which had been shielded by her broken umbrella, was clean, and the jacket hung in gentle folds on either side.

"It's not bad, but what about my hair? And my shoes. I can't go out there with the heel of my shoe missing."

He touched her cheek. "You're on your own with the hair, babe. But I can do something about the shoes. What size?"

"What?"

"What size? There's a department store across the street. They don't close until nine-thirty."

Shayna was dumbfounded. "You're going to buy me new shoes?"

He grinned. "Sure. Why not?"

Shayna sighed. *Why not?* "Well, let me get you some money."

"Forget it. What size?"

"Seven, but—"

"Be right back." He slipped out the door as suddenly as he'd appeared.

She turned back to the mirror. At least this evening

couldn't get any weirder. Ugh. What was she going to do about this hair?

Before Max returned, Shayna managed to retouch her makeup and pull her hair into a respectable French braid with light bangs falling over her forehead. The overall effect wasn't stunning, but it was decent.

Two women had come in to fix their lipstick, when Max strolled in like he belonged there. "Hi, ladies," he said, casually handing Shayna a bag from the shoe store.

She had to laugh when the two women exchanged looks, then hurried out.

Shayna pulled a pair of pearl gray pumps, the exact color of Max's jacket, from the box. "These are beautiful." She slipped them on, feeling like Cinderella.

She turned to the mirror. Not bad. Not bad at all. Maybe this evening would turn out okay after all. She looked at her watch. Nine o'clock. There was still time to find Phillip and—

"Shayna! Watch out!"

Max grabbed her arm and pulled her forward just as a ceiling tile fell right where she'd been standing.

2

Shayna stared into her half-empty glass of white wine, fighting down a yawn. Who would have guessed that Phillip Browning, Jr. was such an incredible bore?

Her eyes had glazed over twenty minutes ago and Phillip had yet to notice. Not once had he asked her a single question about herself or her business. Instead, he stood next to her, droning on about his mention in *Ebony* magazine and his software products.

She couldn't stand another minute of this, Shayna thought, glancing around for an escape route. From his spot at the buffet table, Max caught her eye and raised his glass in a cheerful salute. Shayna raised her glass in return, feeling another guilty twinge for the way she'd shrugged him off outside the ladies' room.

He'd looked out for her tonight, pulling her out of the way before a rain-soaked ceiling tile would have fallen on her. She owed him for that…and more.

Max might not be her ideal dating material, but they definitely had the beginnings of a good friendship. She was just about to go over and tell him so, when Ruth Warner, MBO's president, appeared at the podium for some closing announcements.

"I hope you have enjoyed tonight's mixer. Let's give Lynette Franklin and Ronald Johnson a big round of applause for making tonight a success."

Everyone looked to the back of the room where Lynette and Ronald unclasped hands to wave and smile in response to the applause. The couple had become engaged six months after their first meeting. Lynette was the inspiration for Shayna's eligible bachelors list. If Lynette could find Mr. Right among MBO's membership, why couldn't she?

Shayna glanced sideways at Phillip. *He* was definitely out of the running. How could she get involved with a man who couldn't stop talking long enough to notice her? Thankfully, there were still two more names on her list. Candidate number two, Frederick Montgomery, wasn't present that night, but the successful accountant was very active in the organization. Shayna was certain she'd run into him at the next event, which Ruth had just begun to announce.

"I hope to see you all on Monday night for our annual fund-raiser bake sale. Last year we raised over two thousand dollars. Let's work toward breaking that record this year."

Phillip leaned over to whisper in her ear. "I contributed significantly to last year's profit with my grandmother's award-winning peach cobbler. Ruth asked me to make it again this year," he said proudly.

Shayna smiled politely, darting looks between her

watch and the podium. *Bring it home, Ruth. I can't take much more of this.*

"Enjoy the rest of your evening, ladies and gentlemen, and I hope to see you all Monday night."

The minute Ruth stepped back from the microphone, Phillip started droning again. Shayna bit her lip, feeling trapped.

She felt a hand on her shoulder. "Are you ready to leave?"

She faced Max, showing her relief in her eyes. "As a matter of fact, I am." Turning back to Phillip, she said, "I'm leaving now, but it was...nice talking to you."

"Sure, sure, Shaunice. If you ever need any business software let me know. I'll give you a discount." He winked.

Shayna put her hand on her hip, staring after his retreating form. *"Shaunice?"*

Max took her elbow and began guiding her toward the door. "Don't take it personally. He thinks *my* name is Matt."

She stopped when they reached the hotel lobby. "Thanks for rescuing me, yet again. I guess I'll see you Monday night?"

"How do you plan to get home?"

"I can take a cab."

"Nonsense. I'll give you a ride. You live in Rockville, right? That's on my way."

"You don't have to do that."

"It would be my pleasure."

As they walked down to the parking garage,

Shayna couldn't help admiring Max's profile. She couldn't deny that he was a handsome man. His skin was the color of chestnuts and he had sexy chocolate brown eyes shaped like almonds. It really *was* too bad he wasn't her type, because he was beginning to look better than the topping of an ice cream sundae.

But they couldn't possibly have anything in common. The man made a living playing *video games,* for goodness' sake. She needed someone who could share her appreciation for time and order. Max never showed up for a meeting on time—once he was a day late for a Saturday brunch meeting she'd hosted. She'd bet he didn't even own a calendar. The two of them were such opposites, they'd probably drive each other crazy.

But he *was* sweet.... She had to blink away the image of Max sitting on top of a mound of vanilla ice cream, wearing nothing but hot fudge. She had a weakness for sweets, which is why she only indulged on rare occasion. If she wasn't careful, she'd develop a weakness for Max, and she couldn't indulge in him at all.

He stopped in front of a dark green Pathfinder and her eyes widened. No, it couldn't be. She looked down at the license plate. "This is *your* car." She turned to him, and when she saw the guilt etched on his forehead, she knew for sure.

He held up his hands as if to ward her off. "Look, I'm sorry, Shayna. I was trying to make a yellow light. I couldn't help—"

"It *was* you! I can't believe you were the jerk who

splattered my dress with mud. No wonder you've been so eager to help me out tonight.''

"Now, Shayna, I had no idea that was you until I saw your rain slicker in the bathroom. I came looking for you because I was concerned." He unlocked the passenger door and held it open for her.

Shayna stood outside debating whether or not to get into the truck with him. The night had been such a disaster. It annoyed her that he had a part in it—even if by accident. She'd actually been reconsidering his dating potential. Clearly the chaos of the evening was getting to her.

In the morning she'd wake up in her normal orderly world and everything would make sense again.

Shaking her head, Shayna climbed into the truck. The sooner she got home and got into bed, the sooner this nightmare would be over.

Max took the long route home, hoping to coax Shayna out of her funk before he had to drop her off. He'd been making progress until she saw his Pathfinder. When he offered her a ride, it had never occurred to him that she might recognize his truck. He'd only been thinking of the wistful look he'd caught her sending him from across the room.

When he'd approached her, her honey-colored eyes had gone soft and fluttery. He'd waited six months for Shayna to look at him like that. Now that she had, he wasn't going to blow it over his poor driving manners.

"Are you still awake over there?" he asked. She'd

leaned her head against the headrest and her eyes were closed. "I need directions through your complex."

"Mmm-hmm."

She'd given that same response to all his attempts at conversation. He was fighting a losing battle, but he wasn't about to give up. He had about a minute and a half to turn the evening around. By the time he drove up to her town house, he had an idea.

"I'll walk you to your door," he said, starting to turn off the ignition.

She held up her hand. "That isn't necessary. Here." She handed him three crisp twenty-dollar bills.

"What's this?"

"The money I owe you for the shoes."

He tried to hand it back. "Don't worry about it. Besides, I need to ask *you* for a favor."

"Take the money."

The look in her eyes said she meant business, so he tucked the bills into his shirt pocket.

"Now what can I do for you?" she asked, folding her hands in her lap.

The old Shayna was back—all about schedules and routines. The vulnerable young woman he'd met tonight was well hidden behind a professional veneer.

"Ruth Warner twisted my arm about this bake sale thing, and I ended up promising to bring a chocolate mousse cake."

She raised her brows. "I'm impressed. That's a challenging recipe."

"I know."

"Don't feel bad. Ruth can be persuasive."

"Well, there's only one problem—I can't cook worth a damn."

"Why didn't you tell her that?"

"I told her I might be able to manage a few of those slice-and-bake chocolate-chip cookies, but in two minutes she had me convinced I was underestimating my abilities. A few choice words about public service and a mention in the *Gazette,* and I went from frozen cookie dough to homemade chocolate mousse cake."

Shayna sighed, nodding in sympathy. "I understand. So you want help breaking the news to Ruth, is that it?"

"Actually, I was hoping you'd save my…uh, britches and help me figure out how to cook a cake."

Shayna winced. "You don't 'cook' a cake. You bake it. That's why it's called a bake sale."

"So will you take pity on me?"

She looked up reluctantly, and Max was afraid she would turn him down. "I realize this is short notice. You probably have to bake something yourself."

"Actually, I made my strawberry shortcake yesterday." She gave him a long look, before a small smile bloomed on her lips. "I suppose I can help you out."

"Great." They made arrangements for Shayna to come over the next afternoon, and Max wrote the directions to his house on the back of the bake sale flyer. "I appreciate you helping me out like this."

Her lips curved sweetly. "You were a good friend

to me tonight. Helping you with this cake is the least I can do.'' Her sweet smile turned wicked as she reached for the door handle. ''Even if tonight's disaster *was* partially your fault.''

Max turned to look at her, worried she was still upset. She looked over her shoulder, and he saw her eyes dancing with humor.

''Night, Max.''

''Night, Shayna.'' As he watched her walk to her door, Max smiled, satisfied that the evening was ending on a positive note.

Just as Shayna's foot hit her front step, she went down.

Max was out of the truck and halfway up the walk before she got to her feet. ''Shayna! Are you all right?''

''Yes, yes,'' she said, clutching one of her new shoes to her chest. She brushed away his helpful hands. ''I'm fine, really. Thank you.'' She waved him off as she scrambled on one foot to the door.

After dropping her keys a few times, she finally managed to hobble into the house. Just before the door closed behind her, he heard her swear.

''Damn! That's the second pair of shoes I've ruined tonight.''

Chuckling, Max walked back to his truck. He never would have guessed Shayna was such a klutz.

The earsplitting shrill of her telephone jolted Shayna into consciousness. She reached across her clock radio for the phone, but her fingers only grazed the receiver as she struggled to make sense of the numbers on the digital display—1:38. In the afternoon! She nearly fell out of bed.

As she pulled herself into an upright position, the phone continued to shriek. She grabbed the receiver. "Hello!"

"Shayna? It's Max. Is everything okay?"

"Yes, of course." Never mind that the day was half over and she hadn't gone to aerobics, started her laundry or reviewed the week's client files.

"Good. Then we're still on for this afternoon?"

This *afternoon?* The cake! "Yes, yes definitely."

"Didn't we say one o'clock?"

Her clock now read forty minutes past the hour. "Really? I thought we said two o'clock." Her pride wouldn't allow her to admit that, for the first time in ten years, she'd missed an appointment.

"Oh, okay. I should have known. You know how I am about these things. So I'll see you in twenty minutes."

"I was just on my way out the door."

"Good. See you soon."

Twenty minutes! Shayna stared at her closet in panic. Since she hadn't done her laundry that morning, most of her jeans and casual clothes were still in the hamper. She studied the array of skirts and suits. It was either a suit or...

Her eyes strayed to the workout clothes she'd laid out for the aerobics class she'd missed. She didn't have time to be fashion conscious, and if she showed up in a dress, Max might think she was trying to impress him.

Running for the shower, Shayna washed and dressed in record time. She pulled her hair into a ponytail as she raced down the stairs. After grabbing a dessert cookbook from the pantry, she lifted her keys from the hook.

Shayna smiled down at her watch—1:59. Not bad. She'd be a little late, but Max only lived a few minutes away. Once outside, she scanned the lot for her white Toyota.

That was strange. She usually parked it...

Shayna slammed her palm into her forehead. Her car was still at the service station.

Max looked up from the video game he was working on to check the time. Two-thirty. His brows rose. He'd expected to hear her car pull up right on the dot. But then again, Shayna hadn't been her usual self lately.

Then he heard tires screeching in front of the house. He walked over to the window in time to see a very rumpled Shayna stumble out of a Toyota Camry. By the time he'd climbed the basement stairs and pulled open the front door, she was raising her hand to knock.

She hurried inside then spun on her heel to face him. "I'm so sorry I'm late. I forgot my car was at the service station, and my neighbor Kitty had to—"

He held up his hand to stop her. "It's okay. By my standards, this is right...on time." He couldn't keep his eyes from straying to her hair. Looking away, he tried to repress the grin he felt coming to his lips, but it was already too late.

Following his gaze, Shayna reached up to pat her head. Her ponytail slumped to one side like a fallen tree, and spiky strands were sprouting out all around it. "Oh my goodness. Where's your bathroom?"

He pointed to the top of the stairs, chuckling as she took them two at a time.

As he waited for her to return, Max realized this was yet another side of Shayna he hadn't seen before. Rumpled and mussed, dressed in a faded red sweatshirt, stretch pants and running shoes, she looked comfortable and...cute.

Max grinned. Like she'd just rolled out of bed.

Maybe he'd misjudged Shayna and her rigidity. Sure she was always talking about organization at the meetings, but maybe she *was* more relaxed in her personal life. Perhaps they had more in common than he'd thought.

She came downstairs, looking more like the Shayna he was used to. She'd straightened her ponytail and secured it with one of those bunchies, crunchies or whatever women wore in their hair these days.

He smiled at her. "You didn't have to fix it on my account."

She gave him a sheepish grin that made him want to hug her. "You seem to be catching all my bad hair days."

He reached out to tug on her ponytail. "You always look great to me." As he pulled his hand back, his fingers grazed her neck, and her eyes widened before she dropped her gaze to the floor.

So she felt it, too. Good, Max thought. Now all he had to do was get her to admit it.

Shayna stepped away, nodding as she glanced around. "You have a nice house." Her tone sounded almost surprised.

"Thanks," he said, feeling an uneasy twinge as he realized she probably was.

He knew she didn't have much regard for the fact that he made a living playing video games. She'd probably expected to find him living in a cluttered little shack with plastic furniture and cardboard shelves. He made a good living, and he couldn't resist showing off a little. "Let me show you around."

"Sure," she said, following him upstairs.

By the time they'd made it down to Max's office in the basement, Shayna had given him tips on folding towels, eliminating dust bunnies, and how he could save himself fifteen extra minutes in the morning by switching his socks from the top to the bottom drawer.

"So this is it." Shayna turned around, taking in his office. "This is a nice setup."

Max waited, knowing what was about to follow.

"But you know…"

He grinned. He'd recently learned that all of Shayna's helpful hints began that way.

"If you move your desk over to the window, you could take advantage of the natural sunlight in the morning."

Okay, so she wasn't as laid-back as he'd hoped, and they were as opposite as night and day. That's what Max liked about her.

He knew exactly where she was coming from. He used to be a slave to deadlines and schedules, and he saw so much of his old self in Shayna. Part of him had to admire her devotion to a life-style he hadn't been able to maintain. Another part of him wondered if she would burn herself out the way he had. He knew just what kind of discipline it took to keep up such a rigid pace. He also knew that it eventually took its toll.

Max liked having the freedom to dive off in a new direction the minute an idea surfaced. He'd given up trying to conquer the waves. Now he was content to go with the flow, letting life carry him where it pleased. Would Shayna learn to do the same, or would the currents eventually pull her under?

"Explain to me again how a grown man makes a living playing video games." Shayna was examining the shelves that contained his extensive collection of games and entertainment systems.

"Have you ever played a video game?"

Shayna shrugged. "I played a couple games with my niece at Christmas, but I never really got the hang of it."

"Well, it can be addicting. People—not just kids— are willing to pay a lot of money to someone who can get them through the rough spots. I produce a newsletter that provides hot tips for the latest games, and I have a small staff that mans a video game hot-line.''

Shayna studied the fifty-inch television in the mid-dle of his office. ''Where do you get these tips from?''

He grinned. ''From playing the games.''

She shook her head. ''I don't understand. Isn't that what everybody does? How do you discover these tips no one else can?''

He grinned mischievously. ''It's what I do.''

She shot him an exasperated look.

''Actually, I have an advantage. I used to design video game programs myself. I know what to look for.''

''You used to design video games? You actually wrote the programs?''

He nodded, preparing for her next logical question.

''Then why—''

''Why did I give up designing games to play with them?''

''Yes. Obviously your business is doing well, but programming video games could make you a million-aire. Why would you trade that in?''

''Because of the typical politics that come with big business. To make a long story short, it wasn't fun anymore. The challenge was gone. I enjoy solving the puzzle, finding the quirks and traps in someone else's games. I still knock off a game of my own every now and then, but I'm a free agent, my own boss.''

Her brow was furrowed, as if she were still work-ing it out in her head.

"It's just like you and life management consulting. You took something you had a natural talent for, something you enjoy, and you turned it into a business. It's the same thing. I wanted to be in control, make my own schedule. And most of all, play video games all day."

She raised her eyes and he saw a respect that he'd never seen in those honey-gold depths before. "I do understand. It takes a lot of courage to give up security and take this kind of chance."

He felt a blush creep up his jaw at her unexpected understanding. "Aw, shucks, ma'am." The room became silent. "Why don't we get started with that cake?"

"Right." Shayna sprang into action, heading for the stairs. "Let's see what you have."

In the kitchen, Shayna pulled open the refrigerator, then turned to smirk at him over her shoulder. "This is the typical bachelor's setup. Baking soda, a jar of mustard and beer?"

He shrugged. That's exactly the reaction he'd been going for when he'd emptied the refrigerator last night. He figured she'd judge his culinary skills from the ingredients in his kitchen, and he wasn't going to take any chances on her guessing the truth.

Something told him that Shayna wouldn't be so sympathetic to his situation if she realized he came from a long line of gourmet chefs.

3

Shayna closed Max's refrigerator, shaking her head. This was going to be more of a challenge than she'd realized.

"Okay, Max, we'll have to go to the store. You don't even have the basics. Let me see your recipe so we can figure out exactly what we need."

His brows rose innocently. "Recipe?"

"Yes. Don't you have a… You don't, do you?"

He showed her his straight white teeth, as if flashing that sexy smile would make up for everything. "Well, no."

She grinned. Somehow she just couldn't argue with that smile. "Lucky for you, I grabbed one of my cookbooks on the way out. It's in the car."

He squeezed her shoulder. "You think of everything. I appreciate you helping me out like this."

"No problem." She thought of everything? Yeah, right. She used to think of everything, but today was a different story. She wasn't even sure if the cookbook she'd brought *had* a chocolate mousse cake recipe. There hadn't been time to check. "Let me go get it. I'll be right back."

"Wait. I'll grab my keys and we can leave for the store."

She looked at him in surprise. "But we haven't made a list yet."

Max shrugged. "Why make a list when we already have the cookbook?"

"You want to lug a cookbook around the grocery store with us?"

"We can manage."

Shayna shook her head in confusion. "Max, it only takes five minutes to write out a list."

"It only takes five minutes to drive to the grocery store." He winked at her, leading her into the hallway. "See, I just showed *you* how to save yourself five extra minutes."

Shayna rolled her eyes, realizing that she'd been beaten at her own game. They retrieved the cookbook from her car, then got into Max's Pathfinder.

While she flipped through the cookbook, Max turned on the radio. She was just about to ask him whether he preferred Ultimate Chocolate Mousse Cake or the Chocolate Mocha Mousse Cake, when the chorus to an old Smokey Robinson song came up.

Max sang loud, off-key and with feeling.

Shayna stared at him. He gave her a sympathetic look, but continued to sing with all his heart. When the chorus came up again, he tapped her knee, inviting her to join in. She looked at him in horror.

Max winked, singing even louder.

He hit the high note flat, but it didn't matter. Steering, with one arm, through the light Sunday traffic, he leaned back, fully enjoying the music.

At the end of the song, he turned down the radio and sighed. "Damn, I wish I could sing."

A giggle slipped past Shayna's lips. "You're not the only one." They looked at each other and set off in a fit of laughter.

He began to sing along with the next song, and Shayna had to smile. Despite a strong baritone voice, Max couldn't hit a note with a sledgehammer. But he didn't let that stop him…and that was actually pretty endearing.

Most men she knew would never allow her to see them at such a disadvantage, and they certainly wouldn't be able to laugh at themselves about it. They always had to maintain a veneer of control—the way she did.

The unwanted picture of Phillip Browning, Jr. singing James Brown's "I Feel Good" popped into Shayna's mind, and she almost laughed out loud. Only, in this rendition, he would probably change the word *feel* to *look,* then take credit for writing an original song.

"We're here." Max shifted the truck into park, and as they walked toward the grocery store, he gestured at the slip of paper in her hand. "What's that?"

She felt her cheeks heat. "It's a list. I made it in the car."

He chuckled.

"It won't be as effective because I don't know how

the aisles are laid out in this store. You can save more time if you make your list according to the aisles."

Still chuckling at her words, Max picked out a shopping cart. Shayna couldn't help feeling as though he were laughing at her.

She followed him through the automatic doors. "I know you don't have much reverence for schedules, but they can really make a difference in your life."

Pushing the cart toward the first aisle, Max smiled at her politely. "I believe you. What's the first item on the list?"

"You know..." Shayna said, frowning thoughtfully. "You should let me work up a plan for you. Something simple. Consider it a professional courtesy."

"Uh, Shayna—"

Determined to make him take her seriously, she pressed on. "Really, Max, just think—"

His gaze was fixed beyond her. "Shayna, watch out!"

She turned in time to see a shopping cart careening toward her. Inside was a toddler clapping his hands and shouting, "Whee!" An older boy chased after him.

Trapped between a centerpiece display of eggplant and the orange stand, Shayna had only one choice. She pressed herself against the rows of oranges until she was practically sitting on them. The boys whooshed by.

Her relief was short-lived.

One.

By one.

Oranges.

Began dropping.

To the floor.

Shayna spread her arms, trying to block the falling fruit, but her weight only added to their momentum. Oranges shot out in every direction, rolling down the aisle and under displays.

"Max! Help me!"

Max, who had been standing off to the side, open-mouthed, wheeled the empty shopping cart over to her. "Okay, now slowly step away," he instructed.

She gently eased sideways and the oranges that had been stacked at her back fell into the cart. "What a mess."

Oranges were everywhere. A young woman in a long skirt was hopscotching over the rolling fruit with a carton of milk and a bag of bagels tucked under her arms. At the end of the aisle, the older of the two boys from the shopping cart derby was trying to juggle oranges, while the toddler clapped with glee.

Max darted around the aisle, gathering oranges while Shayna tried restacking the ones that had fallen into the cart. After she'd stacked three oranges, the pile rolled back off. No matter how she tried, the fruit wouldn't stay put.

"What's going on here?" a stock boy asked Shayna just as Max returned with his arms full of oranges.

The mother of the two grocery circus performers

showed up to pull her boys away, leaving Shayna and Max to take the blame.

Shayna tried to stack another orange on the stand. "There was a little accident." The orange rolled off onto the stock boy's foot...followed by three more.

"Aw, man." The teenager reached down to pick up the oranges. "When I applied for this job, they promised me stuff like this only happened on television."

"I'm so sorry." Shayna filled her arms with fruit, trying to help the boy refill the display. He turned suddenly and she spilled her armload all over him.

The boy cursed under his breath, shooing her away. "I'll take care of it. Just go."

Shayna and Max hastily rounded the corner into the next aisle. Feeling her cheeks sting, she motioned to the oranges—at least two dozen—that still layered the bottom of their cart.

Max waved her off, obviously struggling to keep a straight face. "Leave 'em. You can never have too much vitamin C."

"Okay, we've gotten the eggs, butter and cream. All we need now is chocolate." Max steered Shayna toward the candy aisle. She'd refused to handle the eggs because she swore, with her luck, she'd break them all.

"Good." Shayna moaned, eyeing the oranges in their cart, now stored safely in plastic bags. "Then we can leave before I strike again."

Max shook his head warily. She did seem to be

having a rough time of it lately. He'd thought what happened at the mixer last night was a once-in-a-lifetime catastrophe, but since then he'd come to the conclusion that Shayna was just straight-up clumsy.

Until recently she'd always been cool and collected, and it warmed him to see this side of her. He found her clumsiness endearing. But the old Shayna was still alive and well. In between dodging shopping carts and skating on spilled detergent, she'd managed to talk him into buying a pocket planner and changing his brand of toothpaste.

Max picked up the large bittersweet chocolate bar the recipe called for. When he returned to the cart, he found Shayna studying a row of chocolate almond candy bars with open lust.

"Shayna?"

"Hmm?" She faced him with a dreamy, glassy-eyed look.

"If you want a candy bar, just get one."

She bit her lip in obvious distress. "No. I can't."

"Why not?"

"Chocolate is my biggest weakness. I only let myself indulge on special occasions."

Max walked over, picked a candy bar and held it out to her. "Life is too short to be so hard on yourself. If you want something, you have to take it." He waved the candy bar. "Take it."

She turned away. "No. No. No. I try to maintain a well-balanced diet. It would show a terrible lack of discipline for me to give in."

"Shayna, you have a gorgeous figure. One little candy bar isn't going to—"

She turned back, clearly embarrassed. "No, that's not it. I want it too much, and that's why I need to restrain myself. I control the chocolate.... The chocolate doesn't control me."

After a final longing look at the candy bar, she turned and began pushing their cart up the aisle.

"I'll have to remember that," Max said, following behind her.

After filling the cart with all the necessary ingredients, they headed for the checkout line.

"This way," Max said, steering her to the left.

"But, Max, that's the longest line. This one over here is shorter."

He shook his head. "Maybe, but the quality of service isn't the same. Trust me, this lane will be worth the wait."

Shayna eyed the line, making no effort to hide her frustration. "How could any lane be worth a wait this long?"

Max realized the lane was at least twice as long as the others, and Shayna seemed baffled by the fact that no one else seemed to mind. Couples chattered softly among themselves, while others flipped through magazines from the display racks.

As they neared the front, Shayna released another incredulous sigh. She jabbed her elbow into his side. "Max, this woman is the worst," she said, referring to the checkout clerk, a heavyset woman with a short salt-and-pepper Afro. "She's doing more socializing than grocery packing."

He just grinned blithely. "Nah, May Belle's the best. She's the main reason I shop here."

When they reached the head of the line, Shayna looked ready to jump out of her skin. She hastily unloaded their cart, clearly anxious for their shopping excursion to end.

"Well, hi, sugar. How are you doing this afternoon?" May Belle greeted Max with more warmth than some of his relatives at family reunions.

"I'm just fine, May Belle. How are you feeling?"

"Well, now, you know it's been a trial." May Belle started with her aching corns and worked her way up to the chronic pain in her back.

"Hang in there, May Belle."

"Oh, Lord, I do try, but you know how they like to work a poor woman to death up in this place." The sparkle in her eyes said she wouldn't have it any other way. "Enough about me. Let's see what you got here."

Then May Belle's eyes fell on Shayna. "My goodness, boy, why didn't you tell me you finally found yourself a girlfriend? And she's beautiful, too. Don't you two make a handsome couple."

"This is Shayna Gunther, May Belle, and we're just friends. Right now."

Shayna opened and closed her mouth, the color in her cheeks deepening. Max winked at Shayna, enjoying her flustered reaction.

"Nonsense." May Belle leaned toward Shayna.

"Honey, let me tell you something. This boy is the best catch around. And they come from all over to pass through my lane, so May Belle knows. You married?"

"No, ma'am," Shayna squeaked.

"Then, sweetheart, look no farther. Look at him. As handsome as the day is long, sweeter than Mama's homemade pudding, and he can coo—"

"May Belle, please. You're embarrassing me." Max was actually enjoying the attention, but May Belle was about to blow his cover.

"And modest, too. Don't worry, sugar. I've said my piece." She winked at Shayna, returning her attention to the groceries. "My, my, *my,* you got a lot of oranges."

"No, no, Shayna. That's not how you *fold* the egg mixture. That's more of a chopping motion." Max rushed to her side to take over.

She let him take the bowl from her. "I know, but the spatula hits right where I burned myself, and that makes it difficult to …"

"It's okay, I understand. Why don't you grate the… Actually, why don't you sit over there and have a break?"

Shayna slunk over to a chair. "I'm not usually like this, Max. I don't know what's wrong with me. I came over here to help you, and I'm just making a mess of everything."

Max looked over his shoulder at her as he gently

folded the eggs into the chocolate like an old pro. "You're doing fine. We all have days like this."

She watched his effortless motions. "You sure seem to be catching on quick."

"You're a good teacher."

She scoffed. "Yeah, right. So far I've taught you how to burn yourself preheating an oven, ruin batter by dropping hundreds of microscopic eggshells into it, and now you're afraid to let me grate the chocolate because you're thinking I'll scrape off what's left of my fingernails."

Shayna watched glumly as Max carried out the remaining steps of the recipe. Once again he was gliding through life as smooth as silk while she bumped over polyester naps. How could this be?

He could stroll through the store without being distracted by bags of chocolate-chip cookies or almond candy bars. She had to keep both eyes on a list or she'd be overwhelmed by temptation.

How nice it must be to buy things just because you want them. To leave at a moment's notice and arrive without warning. Max, for all his casual disorder and spontaneous chaos, seemed so...free.

Shayna experienced a fleeting moment of envy.

No, she scolded herself. These last few days had proven that when she left one thread unbound, the entire fabric of her life began to unravel.

She sat in Max's kitchen a frazzled wreck because she'd allowed herself to get off schedule—damn that alarm clock. Veering off her routine left her flustered and disoriented. That must explain her clumsiness. High school all over again.

This is what it was like to be out of control—like a derailed train, plowing into oblivion.

She had to get back on track. Fast. Which meant starting a new, more rigorous schedule as soon as possible. Flying by the seat of his pants may work for Max, but it only made Shayna feel dysfunctional.

No matter how adorable Max looked with flour on his jeans and chocolate on his chin, she couldn't be a part of his world. Frederick Montgomery was an accountant. They had an inherent need for order and consistency. That was the kind of man who suited her.

"I can't believe something this delicious only needs to bake for fifteen minutes," Max said, closing the oven door. "Hey, don't sit there looking so depressed."

"I'm fine," Shayna said. "But you have chocolate on your chin." She wanted to wipe it off herself, but she didn't know which she was more afraid of—the chocolate or Max.

He reached up with a paper towel to clean his face. "I know what will cheer you up." He picked up a bowl that had recently been filled with melted chocolate. "Want to lick the bowl?"

Her eyes widened at the thought. "Uh…no. That's unsanitary."

Max studied the bowl critically, then ran his index finger across the bottom. He popped the finger into his mouth and frowned. "You're right. Disgusting!"

He put the bowl into the sink and filled it with water.

Shayna watched the entire process, feeling as though she'd lost her best friend.

"Yep, that was a terrible idea," he said, turning back to her. "I guess I'll just have to be satisfied with this." He reached into his back pocket and pulled out a chocolate almond crunch bar.

Shayna gasped, feeling betrayed. "Where did you get that?"

He grinned slyly. "You were so fascinated with May Belle, you didn't see me slip it in with the other groceries."

"Max! It's not fair of you to eat that thing in front of me."

He peeled back the wrapper, exposing the rich, dark chocolate, then he broke off a chunk. "I'm willing to share."

She caught her breath, feeling her control slipping. What the hell. Today had been a wash anyway. There was always tomorrow.

Her feet had a mind of their own, and she found herself standing in front of him. She reached up to take the chocolate.

Max held it out of reach. "Ah ah ah, we're sharing."

He held the chocolate to her lips until her teeth closed over half of the long chunk. She waited for him to let go, so she could push the rest into her mouth, but before she realized it, his head was dipping. His teeth took hold over the other half. When he bit down, breaking their connection, their lips brushed ever so lightly.

It wasn't quite a real kiss, but to Shayna, it was a taste of the true temptation she'd been fighting all day. She chewed the sweet chocolate in her mouth, but her eyes were locked on the motion of Max's lips.

Suddenly an earlier vision of Max draped in hot fudge flashed through her mind. Heat gathered in her lower body so quickly, she moaned out loud. "Mmm."

Max leaned forward, picking up on her thoughts. "And the chocolate was good, too," he whispered.

Then there was no space between them, and their lips came together with a silent urgency. She felt the smooth skin behind his neck and the spiky hairs at the base of his head with her fingertips. His hands gripped her waist, pulling her closer.

She could still taste the sweet chocolate on his lips, or was it hers? She couldn't tell, and it didn't matter. All she wanted was for the enticing sensations to continue. His heat and his nearness made her burn.

She could feel the fire between them, almost smell the smoke. It was hot. The smoke...*smoke?*

Max broke their kiss with a gasp. "Shayna...I think my kitchen's on fire!"

4

$$\longrightarrow \longleftarrow$$

As it turned out, Max's kitchen wasn't on fire, but Shayna's body was. She busied herself helping Max clean up. Anything to keep her mind off their recent kiss.

Max dumped the smoking cake pan into the sink. "Maybe we can still salvage this. We can jack up the price and sell it as chocolate mousse flambée, or blackened mousse cake, Cajun-style."

"Sorry, Max," Shayna said, pinching her nose against the lingering smell of burned chocolate. "I'm afraid you're going to have to start over from scratch."

She scrubbed out the oven where chocolate had bubbled over onto the rack, while Max trudged back to the grocery store for fresh supplies.

After throwing out the ruined cake, she washed the dishes and wiped the countertops until they sparkled, but the memory of Max's kiss remained on her lips. A sponge and soap weren't enough to scrub away her desire to have his arms around her again.

Shayna sat at the kitchen table, tracing the simple pattern on the tablecloth. She wanted a relationship.

She was actively seeking one, and as far as men went, Max was great. Why did the idea of what was happening between them scare her so badly? Sure, he wasn't on her list of suitable bachelors, but if she had to make a list of scorching kissers, Max would be at the top.

Confused, Shayna popped up from the table. She needed to stay busy. The dish rack was piled high with at least three days' worth of dishes, in addition to cake pans and mixing bowls. She decided to help Max out by putting some away. Maybe she could even give him a hand reorganizing his shelves.

Pulling open the silverware drawer, she found a myriad of forks, knives, spatulas and spoons thrown haphazardly inside. She cringed. "How does he live like this?"

Shaking her head, Shayna began to sort Max's mismatched flatware into the appropriate slots. She frowned when she came across a collection of plastic "sporks" with Colonel Sanders's head stamped on the handles. Wrapping a rubber band around them, she hid them in the back of the drawer.

"This man needs serious help." She could picture him setting a dinner table for clients with his Batman and Robin jelly glasses and his colorful plastic all-star basketball dishes.

Shayna laughed at the thought. Max was cute, but he just didn't take life seriously enough. Look how one day in his presence had eroded her common sense. Spending more time with him might make today's fluster a permanent condition.

She started opening cabinets, looking for a place to put Max's Washington Redskins coffee mug. An odd shape under a dustcover on the top shelf of his pantry caught Shayna's eye. Curiosity got the best of her as she dragged over a step stool. It would be just like Max to keep power tools of some sort in the kitchen.

Balancing on the stool, Shayna lifted the edge of the dustcover, expecting to find a belt sander or some other ill-placed masculine contraption. A glimpse of white plastic had her pulling the dustcover all the way off. She stared in shock. What was Max doing with a pasta maker?

Could it be a gift? But why dump a gourmet appliance on someone who didn't know the difference between cooking and baking a cake? Shayna peeked into the cardboard box next to the pasta maker.

Surprised, she pulled it off the shelf and set it on the kitchen table. She began pulling out expensive copper pots, a garlic press, a lemon squeezer, stainless-steel colanders, a four-sided grater and a pepper mill. These were some gourmet utensils for someone who didn't know how to cook.

Hands on her hips, Shayna tapped her foot on the kitchen tile. She glanced from the chocolate cake remains in the garbage to the box of cooking utensils on the table. "I smell a setup," she said through clenched teeth.

A few moments later, when Max walked through his front door with an armload of groceries, Shayna was waiting for him in the front hall with a copper pot in one hand and a stainless-steel whisk in the other.

She arched her brow and affected a Ricky Ricardo accent. "Max, you got some 'splaining to do!"

Brows raised in question, Max edged past Shayna into the kitchen. He stopped short when he saw his cooking utensils spread over the kitchen table. Setting down the groceries, he turned around with his hands up.

"Okay, I'll take my punishment like a man," he stated as Shayna advanced on him like Betty Crocker on a mission. "Are you going to clock me over the head with that pot and then whisk me to death?"

"Maybe," she said, waving the whisk in the air. "What is a man who doesn't know how to cook doing with an expensive collection of cookware and a pasta maker, for heaven's sake?"

He hunched his shoulders, not even trying to look sincere. "Would you believe they were housewarming gifts?"

"No." She held up the copper pot and moved toward him. "But I would believe you set me up. You told me you didn't know how to bake, just to get me over here. You manipulated me, then used my weakness for chocolate against me."

His lips quirked. "It really wasn't as premeditated as it sounds."

"Oh, yeah? What did you do with the food?"

"What food?"

"Come on, you must have emptied out the refrigerator. What did you do with the food?" There was no way a man with this kind of cookware existed on the pathetic scraps she'd found in the refrigerator. He must have tossed it out before she came over.

A guilty look crossed his face. "Okay, it was a little premeditated, but let me explain."

"Why should I? You lied to get me over here. Why should I believe anything you have to say? You clearly have a hidden agenda."

He moved the box to a countertop and pulled out a kitchen chair. "Shayna, please sit down. Let me take those," he said, disarming her of the kitchen weaponry. "From what I've seen of you around here today, a copper pot in your hands is almost as dangerous as a loaded gun."

She let go of the utensils but she didn't sit down. "Oh, so you think this is funny?"

"No, I don't. But I was sort of hoping you would. Okay, the jokes aren't working. I guess that means I'm going to have to come clean." He rubbed the back of his neck. "This isn't easy."

Shayna sank into the chair feeling wary and emotionally exhausted. When had her nice tidy life gotten so confusing? She rubbed her temple. "Out with it, Max. Now."

"It's simple really. Shayna, I have a crush on you."

Shayna felt her jaw fall open. That was the last thing on earth she'd expected him to say. "A crush? Max you sound like you're in high school."

In high school, hunky guys like Max didn't get crushes on Shayna. Only the studious reclusive types had the nerve to come near her. The last time a handsome jock had tried to ask her out, she'd accidentally dropped a thick volume of *Twentieth-Century World History* on his foot, crippling him before the last basketball game of the season.

"Shayna, I *feel* like I'm in high school when I'm around you." He leaned against the edge of the table next to her chair. "My palms get sweaty and my mouth goes dry. Ever since I walked into my first MBO meeting six months ago and saw you sitting there looking beautiful and unapproachable, it's been high school all over again. I've tried to talk to you, but up until last night, you were merely polite. I knew I didn't have a chance."

He crossed his arms over his chest. "Last night I saw a side of you I'd never seen before."

Shayna shuddered, remembering her hair à la Don King and dress by Drowned Rat. "No kidding."

"No, I don't mean that," Max said, laughing. "I mean you were vulnerable and sweet, and for about five minutes I actually thought you felt a spark of attraction, too."

Shayna looked away. A spark? If that's what happened when you threw a match in a case of dynamite—then, yes, she'd felt a spark.

"Then, on the drive home, you started shutting down on me again. Polite and professional. It was as though you'd put on a business suit and tied your hair back in a bun."

Professionalism was safe; the thoughts she'd been having had not been.

"I hated losing that easy rapport we'd fallen into, so I acted on impulse. Like a high school kid, I came up with this crazy idea that if you helped me bake this cake, we could spend more time together. You could get to know me and might realize that I'm not such a bad guy after all."

"Max," Shayna protested, "I never thought you were a bad guy."

"Okay, but you *do* know about that frosty look you have that tells all men within a thousand-mile radius to back off."

Shayna felt a rush of heat sting her cheeks. She *could* be a bit frosty on occasion.

"But today, you let your guard down. We had a few hairy moments, but all in all I think we had fun."

She nodded slowly.

"Look, Shayna, I know it was a crazy thing to do. I didn't want to make you feel manipulated or used." His dark eyes searched hers imploringly. "Let me make it up to you. I'll get the porterhouse steaks and ice cream I stashed in my neighbor's fridge, and I'll whip up the best dinner I know how to make."

Shayna cracked a little smile. Resisting those rueful eyes took more energy than she had. But that didn't mean she couldn't make him sweat it out a few more minutes.

"Your neighbor's refrigerator, huh? So that's where you hid the food. Just how well *can* you cook? You owe me big time for injuries earned in the line of duty." She held up the finger she'd burned on the oven.

Max looked relieved. "How well can I cook?" He gave her a sheepish look and went to the pantry, coming back and dropping a thick blue bound cookbook on the table. "That's Grandfather Winston's."

He dropped two more on top. "Those two are my dad's. I may have betrayed my lineage by going into computer games instead of becoming one of the greatest chefs on the East Coast, but at least my elders made sure I could cook my pants off."

Shayna spread out the books and read the titles aloud. "*Real Soul Food*, by Chef Grover Winston. *Great Chefs of the Capital City. Chef Maxwell Winston Presents Great American Soups.* Impressive." She glanced up at him. "Okay, Winston, I want to see magic. This meal had better live up to your family name."

Max had, indeed, been holding out on her. The steak he'd served had been incredibly tender and seasoned exquisitely. But that alone had not won her over. Every man knew how to grill a steak, right? The real tribute to the Winston family name had been the Caesar salad, with dressing he made from scratch—crumbled blue cheese, balsamic vinegar, fresh grated Romano cheese and croutons he toasted from crunchy French bread.

After dinner, Max cleared away the dishes and placed the second chocolate mousse cake in the oven. He returned to the table with two bowls of vanilla ice cream topped with real maple syrup and crushed walnuts.

Shayna patted her tummy. "I have to admit, I was

skeptical, but now I can say that was the best meal I've eaten in a long time. I didn't think I would like cold soup,'' she said, referring to the appetizer—tomatoes whisked in a blender, laced with light sour cream, seasoned with thyme and basil then served cold.

Max dipped his spoon into his ice cream and raised an eyebrow. ''Does this mean you forgive me?''

''Mmm,'' she said coyly. ''Let me think.'' She slipped the first spoonful of ice cream into her mouth, savoring the cool sweetness. ''On top of everything else, you have excellent taste in ice cream. I think I'm going to have to forgive you.''

''Whew!'' He wiped imaginary sweat from his brow. ''You had me worried for a while there.''

Shayna continued to eat her ice cream, enjoying the indulgence. She'd already spoiled her diet for the day, so she decided to make it count. It was all she could do not to moan with pleasure after each bite.

She studied the bowl thoughtfully. ''Ice cream can't possibly taste this good to everyone. If so, people would eat nothing else.''

She took another spoonful, letting it slide slowly into her mouth. ''I read somewhere that denying the body certain pleasures, such as sweets, intensifies the experience. It must be true because eating this ice cream is like…'' She paused when she noticed Max's eyes locked on her lips.

His spoon was poised over the bowl and his ice cream was forming a growing puddle in his dish.

She licked her lips self-consciously and saw his lips

part with an audible huff. When he finally realized she was watching him watch her, his spoon clattered into the bowl.

Shayna dug into the dessert with renewed relish, trying to pretend she hadn't seen the blatant desire on his face. Max wasn't going to let her get away with that.

The light touch of his fingers brushing her wrist almost sent her rocketing out of her chair.

"Shayna, you never told me how you feel about what I said to you earlier."

Heat burned a trail up her neck as panic set in. Her eyes looked everywhere but at him. "I think it's wonderful that you come from a long line of chefs."

He blew out his breath in frustration. "You know that's not what I mean. I'm attracted to you, Shayna. After that kiss, I don't think you can deny that the feeling is mutual."

Shayna squirmed in her seat. "Max, about that kiss—"

His grip tightened on her arm and his touch set off mini-explosions of sensation under her skin. "If you're about to tell me that kiss was a mistake, don't bother. I know you don't believe that."

She twisted in her seat, gently tugging her arm away from his fingers. How could he expect her to think straight with him touching her? "Okay, Max, you're right. Maybe there is something between us."

"Maybe?"

"Okay, there *is* something between us. But we can't let it go any further."

"Why not?"

How could she explain about her list of eligible bachelors without sounding like a nut? Max already thought she was a bit off for planning each detail of her life down to her pale yellow bikinis. She needed a man she had things in common with.

Max threw her off balance. He didn't understand the importance of organization to a comfortable lifestyle. How could she get involved with a man who shook up her system this much?

His fingers found her wrist again, silently pressing her to continue as his thumb caressed her tender skin. How could she *not* get involved with a man who shook up her system *this* much?

"Max, you're a great guy—"

A deflated sigh escaped his lips, and he pulled back his hand. She immediately missed his touch. He shook his head, sinking down in his chair. "This is the old, 'You're a great guy, but let's just be friends' speech. It's okay, Shayna, you don't have to say any more."

"No, wait." Shayna grabbed *his* arm this time. "You don't understand."

His brows rose. "I understand that you're not willing to give me a chance."

She pulled her hand back to press her fingers to her lips. "But, Max, it's nothing personal—"

He looked at her as though she were on heavy medication. "Are you kidding me?"

"I mean, I do like you and I'm attracted to you, but…you're just not my type."

He picked up his bowl of melted ice cream and dumped it in the sink. "I've seen your type, Shayna. Believe me, you're not missing anything."

"Okay, Max, exactly what do you think is my type?"

He faced her. "Wears designer suits, carries a cell phone, gets his hair cut twice a week—all because image is everything. He does that whole corporate America thing, so one day he can have a country home in Virginia. Intelligent, professional, has the right look, the right attitude. All he's missing is the right woman to settle down with. How am I doing?"

She had to hand it to him. Eligible bachelors one, two and three could all fit that description. "Not bad."

"Of course it's not bad, Shayna. I used to *be* that guy."

Before she could stop it, a laugh bubbled up from her throat. "You? I don't believe it."

"No, honestly. That was me. Doing the nine to five. Working the system. Climbing the ladder. The whole nine yards."

Part of Shayna still thought he was joking. "Oh, yeah. Then what changed you?"

A shadow passed over his face and he turned away, picking up a dishrag to wipe around the sink. When he finally spoke, his voice lacked its usual spirit. "Let's just say I woke up before it was too late."

Shayna frowned. There was a story here.

Then he turned around and gave her a little grin.

"Why do you have to cross me off your list so quickly?"

A blast of cold fear struck her. "List? What list? I don't know what you're talking about."

"You know what I mean. Why do you have to throw me out of the running? Kick me out of the game. Don't write me off so easily."

Shayna resisted the temptation to grip her chest in relief. He didn't know about her eligible bachelors list.

"Can't you give us some time to get to know each other—even if it's just as friends first—then see what happens after that?"

"Oh, I...can't think straight." She rubbed her forehead. "It's been such a long day. I guess so."

He nodded. "It is getting late. All I'm asking is that you think about it. Consider giving me a chance."

"Okay," she said as he walked her to the door.

Self-consciously she dug into her purse for her keys, not wanting to meet his eyes. Immediately her breath mints, lipstick, Tylenol and compact clattered to the floor. Max helped her pick everything up.

Shayna was ready to make a mad dash for her car. "Well, I guess I'll see you tomorrow night at the bake sale?"

"I'll be there." He moved closer to her. "Can I at least have a kiss good-night?"

She didn't protest when his head began to descend toward hers. Closing her eyes, she gave herself up to the moment. She could worry about the consequences

tomorrow. His lips had just made the barest of contact
with hers when a violent buzzing jolted them apart.

The smoke alarm.

They looked at each other and shouted in unison.
"The cake!"

5

Monday evening, Shayna walked into the multipurpose room of Lake Forest Elementary School with a perfect strawberry shortcake. She was thirty minutes early, and she'd even remembered to pick up Max's jacket from the dry cleaner. It was the least she could do after he'd so generously lent it to her.

With the plastic dry-cleaner bag folded over her arm and her cake balanced in the other hand, Shayna searched the room for a safe place for both items.

It felt good to get back to her normal self. At some point over the weekend, she'd slipped into the Twilight Zone, but now she was back in the real world.

It was amazing what a good night's sleep could do. She'd had three clients that day and each consultation had run smoothly. One client had even given her a referral that could turn into several months' worth of new business. She'd found some new high-protein recipes in her latest fitness magazine, and she'd planned out a well-balanced menu for the entire week. Her orderly life was back in sync and, best of all, she was having a good hair day.

She reached up to touch the sleek hair curving into

her face. She'd had to go for the Naomi Campbell look again just to prove it could be done. Besides, Frederick Montgomery would be here tonight. It wouldn't go to waste.

"Shayna, you look great." Lynette Franklin came up from behind her. "Is that a new hairstyle?"

"Yes, thank you. I'm trying something a little different."

Lynette squeezed her shoulder. "It suits you, and look at that strawberry shortcake. I might have to put a bid on that one myself." She turned and pointed to a long table behind her. "We changed the layout this year. The cookies and pastries are at the front and the cakes and pies are back there."

"Okay. Once I put everything down, I'll help you set up."

Shayna started toward the back table, stopping midstride to examine the crest on her whipped cream. It was starting to deflate. She studied it, wishing she'd brought extra topping for a last-minute touch-up.

Just then, a man backing away from the cake table veered into her path, nearly knocking her down. Shayna teetered on her heels, bobbing the shortcake from hand to hand, trying to regain her balance. His arms reached out to steady her.

"I'm sorry about that. I didn't see you standing there. Are you okay?"

Shayna blinked as she found herself staring into the eyes of Frederick Montgomery. Eligible bachelor number two. "I'm fine, but that was a close one. Your suit was in serious jeopardy. I almost dumped this shortcake all over you.''

With manicured fingers, he straightened his dark suit, flashing a charming smile. ''That's okay. It was entirely my fault. Besides, I have a weakness for strawberries.''

Shayna laughed, taking in Frederick's cap of wavy curls. The diamond stud in his ear contrasted with an otherwise conservative package. This was it. Now that she had him all to herself, she had to make it count.

''So…where's your contribution?'' She'd never been good with witty repartee.

''I put it on the wrong table and was just going back to get it.'' His dark gold eyes lowered, and he leaned in closer as though he were about to confide a secret. ''I made a white chocolate cheesecake with fresh strawberry topping.''

''That sounds incredible. Why don't we trade cakes right now?''

His gaze swept over her with masculine appreciation. ''Well, I'll let you try mine, if you let me try yours.''

She smiled. The line was a bit corny, but it was a start. ''Sounds yummy.''

Shayna approached the cake table again. This time, she got three feet away only to pause when she heard someone call her name. She turned and all thoughts of Frederick Montgomery flew from her head. Max was approaching her with two cakes, one balanced on each palm.

It had been eighty-five degrees outside that day and

Max was wearing jean shorts and a red T-shirt. Not at all the appropriate attire for such an event. Still, she felt her mouth grow dry as she gaped openly. The material stretched over his chest, outlining the firm body that lay beneath.

"Max." Shayna was jolted back to her senses when she heard the husky way she'd half moaned his name. "Two cakes?" she asked, trying to cover her fascination with his pectoral muscles, not to mention those long athletic legs.

He grinned, making her heart toss in her chest. "Yeah, I finally finished chocolate mousse cake number three around ten-thirty last night." He winked, reminding her of what they'd been doing that had gotten the first two cakes burned to a crisp. "Then, this morning, I had some free time, so I decided to make an orange tart with half a dozen oranges I just happened to have on hand."

Shayna giggled. With Max, it was suddenly a little bit easier to laugh at herself. In high school, she'd had no sense of humor about her ill-fated incidents. Max made her minor catastrophes seem like a private joke.

"That was clever. I guess I'll have to think of something interesting to make with my half of the oranges."

"I have another orange tart at home that I'd be happy to share. Why don't you bring over whatever you come up with and we can have a little...taste test?"

The way he pronounced the word *taste* sent memories of Max's lips—their taste and texture—flashing through her brain. She almost swayed on her feet.

"Shayna?" asked a deep voice from behind her. "I thought you were headed for the cake table."

Frederick! And here she was about to swoon over Max. *Get your priorities straight, Shayna!*

Taking a deep breath, she spun around to face him, realizing too late that her heel had become tangled in the plastic dry-cleaner bag dangling from her arm. Fighting for balance, she clutched the cake in both hands. Her whole body pitched forward, connecting with something solid. A man's chest. She and Frederick went down, their cakes squashed between them.

"Oh my goodness." She immediately scrambled to her feet and watched, horrified, as Frederick Montgomery rose in front of her.

She reached out to him, searching for the words to express her apologies, embarrassment and regret, but his attention was focused on his clothes. Strawberries, whipped cream and cheesecake smeared his shirt and pants.

"This is a six-hundred-dollar suit! What kind of idiot—" He caught himself before he could finish that thought. He scraped the thick cheesecake from his suit and flicked it off his hands.

Shayna reeled back as cake splattered her panty hose and shoes.

"Look, buddy, it was an accident," Max protested on her behalf.

Shayna's heels lost traction on a heap of strawberry filling and slid out from under her. She fell back into

Max like a bowling ball, knocking them both off their feet.

The two cakes in Max's hands flipped into the air and came down on his head and chest.

"Oh, no!" She slapped her hands to her forehead, realizing too late that her hands were covered with whipped cream. She grabbed a scrap of fabric to clean her face, only to discover with horror that she'd just used Max's freshly cleaned jacket as a towel.

Frederick gave her a look of pure disgust and stalked away.

Shayna looked up to find a crowd of MBO members standing on the sidelines. Some were laughing. Others stood gaping in disbelief.

Lynette rushed over, helping Shayna to her feet. "Are you all right?"

She nodded, looking down at Max who had mousse cake dripping from his face. She watched a smile crack the wall of chocolate and icing. He reached down and dipped his finger into the whipped cream on his shirt and popped it into his mouth.

"I've got to hang out with you more often, Shayna. I can never tell what's going to happen next."

Shayna stumbled into her home, pain thumping at her temple. The evening had been a nightmare.

She dragged herself up the stairs, reaching blindly for the light switch as she groped for the bathroom medicine cabinet. She tapped two white pills onto her palm and downed them with water. Stripping out of her clothes, she pulled her terry-cloth robe from the hook behind the bathroom door. Shrugging into it, she tried to block out the mortifying disaster she'd created at the elementary school.

Four cakes had been destroyed and Max's jacket had been stained beyond repair. Frederick Montgomery wouldn't even look her in the eye and, worst of all…she didn't care.

What was happening to her life? She slunk out of the bathroom, heading straight for her large four-poster bed. Before she could sink into the comfort of her overstuffed pillows, the phone rang. Shayna ignored it, falling back on the mattress. She covered her eyes with her arm.

If that was Ruth Warren calling to revoke her MBO membership, she didn't want to hear it.

The phone rang again. If that was a client calling to fire her, it could wait.

The machine picked up and her recorded voice began speaking. If that was eligible bachelor number three, Jason McKnight, calling to ask her not to bother pursuing him because he'd heard she was a walking disaster, she didn't want to hear that, either.

"Shayna, this is Nicole. I was just calling to finalize our plans for Tiffany to spend the weekend, but I guess you're not home…."

Shayna rolled across the bed and stretched for the phone. "I'm here, Nicole."

"You sound out of it. It's only nine o'clock. Were you sleeping?"

"No. I've just had a bad day. A couple of bad days, really. Make that a bad week."

"How could you have had a bad week? It's only Monday." She could hear the smile in her sister's voice.

"If only you knew."

"Give me a hint."

"Okay, since Friday I have had multiple car troubles. I ruined two pairs of shoes and was nearly decapitated by a wet ceiling tile. I unleashed an avalanche of oranges in a grocery store aisle, helped burn two chocolate mousse cakes and tonight I turned the MBO bake sale into a food fight."

A long stretch of silence followed Shayna's breathless confession. Then a giggle. And a snort. And finally a rumbling guffaw built into a long, roaring belly laugh.

"You're joking, right? Did all that really happen?" Nicole asked, catching her breath.

Shayna pressed her head into the pillow and sighed pitifully.

"Wait a minute. Those things really *did* happen?"

"I seem to have fallen into some alternate universe where down is up and right is wrong. I just can't seem to get it together lately."

Nicole kicked into sympathetic older-sister mode. "We all hit rough patches every now and then, Shayna. Remember my honeymoon with Edmund? That roach-infested shack that was supposed to be a tropical paradise, and bailing Ed out of jail on our wedding night? It was a nightmare, but our second honeymoon was perfect. Things will get better."

"I don't know. I've been walking under a storm

cloud lately. I may drown in rain before the sun shines again.''

''Hang in there, kid. Just don't mention any of this to Tiffany when we drop her off this weekend. She'll be convinced her little chain letter had something to do with it.''

''Chain letter?'' Shayna caught her breath. ''Oh my goodness, I'd forgotten about that.''

''Girl, don't go getting superstitious on me now. I'm having a heck of a time convincing Tiffany not to believe in things like that.''

After hanging up the phone, Shayna piled her long hair on top of her head, envisioning a long bath with scented bubbles. Unfortunately, it would take more than a little hot water to wash away her problems.

She walked past her office, then backed up, pausing in the doorway. Her eyes locked on the recycling bin. The chain letter. She bit her lip. Maybe it wouldn't hurt to just—

Oh, no. Shayna spun on her heel and locked herself in the bathroom. She was *not* superstitious. She did not believe in chain letters. Sure, she'd run into a little bad luck lately, but it had nothing to do with some silly chain letter. Right?

Turning on the water faucet, she picked up her aromatherapy foam bath but, after knocking her favorite earrings into the toilet, breaking a bottle of nail polish and cutting her big toe on the glass, Shayna abandoned all hope of a long hot soak.

She limped out of the bathroom. She couldn't possibly be this clumsy on her own. There had to be some kind of cosmic intervention, she thought, walking back into her office.

Reaching down, she dragged the recycling bin out from under her desk. Despite herself, she glanced over her shoulder. She knew no one could see her, but she couldn't help the automatic action. It wouldn't hurt to *read* through the letter again—just to check it out. She wouldn't actually follow through.

Without further hesitation, she began sorting through old invoices, memos and letters. She ignored the painful paper cut that slit her palm. Finally she retrieved the wrinkled notebook paper with Tiffany's large pencil print.

This is not a joke or a prank. It is very serious. If you follow these instructions carefully, you will find true love.

True love? Shayna laughed out loud, thinking of Phillip Browning, Jr. and Frederick Montgomery. If these last few days had taught her anything, they taught her that she didn't know the first thing about true love. Those men should have been perfect for her. They both had so much in common with her, such as similar backgrounds and goals for the future. There had just been one little problem: they were both tremendous losers.

Jason McKnight was her last shot. He was it. She had no other resources. Jason owned a small restaurant and nightclub on the edge of Washington, D.C. She'd actually had a few conversations with him, and she was pretty certain he wasn't as self-involved as Phillip or a temperamental jerk lacking a sense of humor, like Frederick. But he'd been last on her list because she wasn't sure about his stability. A night-club owner probably kept an erratic schedule.

She also didn't know if he could kiss. Suddenly that had become an important item on her list of must haves. Max may not run a conventional business with regular hours and a set routine, but he definitely knew how to kiss. His kisses were so hot, they melted her like chocolate, sweet and— What was it about that man and chocolate? Here she was with a terrible weakness for the stuff, and he kept managing to get himself covered in it. He wasn't playing fair. How could she resist a man whose kisses were literally more intoxicating than her biggest vice? This evening his face had been layered with chocolate mousse cake, and she'd missed the opportunity to lick it directly—

A hot blush ended that train of thought.

Max had been the only person to maintain a sense of humor about the whole incident. He'd laughed as though sliding around in cake filling was the best fun he'd had in years.

Shayna realized with a jolt that she was staring wistfully off into space. She glanced back down at the wrinkled chain letter in her hand.

Within seventy-two hours, you must copy this letter six times and mail it to six friends who are looking for love.

She wasn't really going to do this, was she? Not only had her time limit expired, the very idea was ridiculous. Tossing the letter onto her desk, she knelt down to push the recycling bin back into place. She banged her knee on the way down and cracked her head backing out from under the desk.

She got back up, favoring her toe, clutching her knee and rubbing her scalp. Maybe it wouldn't hurt to go ahead and make the copies. She wouldn't need them, but they'd be there just in case.

Six letters, huh? Throwing reason to the wind, she tucked the letter into her fax machine and hit the copy button. She pulled out six envelopes. Here came the tough part. She didn't plan to actually mail the letters, but just in case, she ought to at least pick her targets.

The first two were easy. She knew two very eligible bachelors who deserved a shot at true love. With good old Phil and Fred taken care of, she still had four letters left. She'd be humiliated if anyone she knew found out she had done this.

Then she was struck by inspiration. Chain letters were for teenage girls. They might even have fun with them. Before Shayna's consulting business had taken off, she'd done a lot of baby-sitting for her neighbors. She knew at least four teenage girls who could put a chain letter to good use.

Sealing the last of the prestamped envelopes, Shayna dropped the six letters into her Out bin. She'd done enough for one night. By morning, her life would probably find perspective again, and she could tear them up and move on.

Comforted by that thought, Shayna turned out the light and went to bed.

At midnight, on the third day, drink a glass of water and say the name of a boy or girl you like. He or she will be yours forever. If you break the chain, beware. Bad luck will be yours. Forever.

Shayna stared at the chain letter through bleary eyes, no longer caring about superstition or feeling foolish. She just wanted someone to put her out of her misery.

It was Wednesday night and her computer had crashed, causing her to lose a week's worth of work in just seconds. She could see six crisp white envelopes still haunting the bottom of her Out bin. They were now buried under a mountain of correspondence that she'd just spent hours laboriously restoring in her computer.

Without the strength or presence of mind to fight it any longer, Shayna gathered up six hours' worth of work and six chain letters and carried them out to the mailbox.

Feeling drained enough to sleep where she stood, Shayna glanced at her watch—11:53.

Shaking her head, she trudged into the kitchen. "Okay, okay, I give up. Let's just get this over with."

She took her time filling a tall glass with fresh ice cubes and spring water. She swirled the water, watching the ice clink against the frosty glass. It was 11:57.

"Okay, Jason McKnight, lucky bachelor number three, looks like you are the winner. Shayna, why don't you tell him what he's won?"

She propped her hip against the kitchen counter, speaking into her glass as though it were a microphone. "Well, Mr. McKnight. You've won the unique opportunity to wine and dine Shayna Gunther, thereby proving to her that all men are not pathetic losers, and that she has done the right thing in not swearing off dating altogether."

She caught her reflection in the microwave. Her hair flew out at all angles from constant raking, and her eyes were glossy with fatigue. "My goodness, I've really lost it, haven't I?"

Eleven fifty-nine. "Well, Jason, here goes nothing."

Her watch beeped when the hour struck midnight, and Shayna raised the water glass to her lips. Draining it quickly, she saluted the air. "Maxwell Winston."

Her arm froze in midair the second she realized what she'd actually said. "Wait a minute! Can I take that back? I meant to say midnight—I mean McKnight. Jason...oh, shoot!" She stamped her foot and the frosty glass slid through her fingers and shattered on her kitchen floor.

6

Shayna was right about one thing, Max thought. Moving his desk over to the window *did* allow him to take advantage of the morning sunshine, but it also gave him one more reason not to concentrate on his work.

Let's see… Should he stare at the growing mound of paperwork covering every flat surface within reach or at his lawn that needed mowing? How could he chain himself to his desk, slaving over unwritten game reviews and business letters when the seventy-five-degree weather was perfect for a cookout?

Max turned off his computer. He couldn't. That was the advantage of self-employment. He could work anytime, and if he wanted to take the day off to enjoy the weather, he could do that, too.

He was in the mood to fire up the grill but, as he climbed the basement stairs, he realized barbecuing for one was pretty pointless. Max stroked the stubble on his chin, wondering what Shayna had planned for the weekend. If he invited her over, she'd probably turn him down. Knowing her, she'd sit behind her desk, doggedly churning out faxes, E-mail and letters until the sun set.

He couldn't let that happen. She'd schooled him on how to best appreciate the morning sunlight; now he could return the favor. Max grinned. Then maybe their next lesson would involve candlelight....

Stepping out onto the deck, Max leaned against the railing to think. How could he convince Shayna to pay him a visit?

He thought back to last week's Friday night in the ladies' room of the hotel. She hadn't returned the jacket he loaned her. These days he rarely had use for suit jackets, and when he did, he had a closet full of expensive suits he could wear, but Shayna didn't know that. He could ask her to bring it over. Then once he got her inside...well, who could pass up the inviting smell of hamburgers sizzling on a grill?

Max nodded, satisfied with his plan. He had a mission. There was no mistaking it: Shayna was a sexy woman, and he'd love their friendship to move to the next level—but he also worried about her high stress level.

She hadn't taken him seriously the other day when he'd told her he used to live a different life-style. He'd done such a good job of transforming his habits and work ethics, she couldn't imagine him any other way. But two years ago, he and Shayna would have had a lot in common. The strict confines she'd crammed her life into were similar to the ones he'd walked—no—*run*—away from, and he'd never looked back.

He couldn't stand by and watch her make herself a slave to the madness of her schedules and routines. She needed to relax, to have fun. Shayna took life far too seriously.

Max reached for the telephone. She didn't know it yet, but Max was going to loosen Shayna up, whether she liked it or not.

"I'm bored, Aunt Shay!"

Those four words had haunted Shayna all morning. What had happened to the excited little girl who had been so happy to see Shayna when Nicole and Edmund had dropped Tiffany off last night? They'd made dinner together, watched a video and talked about boys just as she'd done at slumber parties as a child.

By now, the novelty had clearly worn off. Tiffany woke up Saturday morning cranky and perpetually bored. Shayna had prepared an entire list of activities for them, but she was learning quickly that little girls didn't respond well to schedules.

Worst of all, Shayna had tossed and turned all night, just as she had the night before. Max hadn't left her thoughts since she'd completed that stupid chain letter two days ago.

She'd been tired. It had been a long day. So what if she'd said his name by accident. It didn't— *couldn't*—mean anything.

"Aunt Shay! I don't feel like playing Scrabble anymore."

"That's okay, Tif. We can do something else." She started putting away the board game.

Okay, maybe saying Max's name *did* mean something. It meant she'd let him get under her skin, that's all. She'd been out of the dating game for a while and, despite her best efforts, Max was the only man she'd spent time with lately. Of course, he'd be on her mind. All she needed was a little de-Maxing.

Tiffany flopped onto her back. "Let's *do* something."

Shayna looked down at her watch. "It's only eleven-thirty but I guess we can make lunch now. I was hoping you'd like to play some board games for a while longer. Then we can go outside. There's a park down the street—"

"I'm not hungry. And it's too hot outside. What else can we do?"

Heaving in a calming breath, Shayna studied Tiffany's prone form. Arms flailed to one side, legs twisted to the other, Tiffany's head was thrown back at an angle as she stared at the ceiling. Her eyes had practically rolled back in her head. It would seem Shayna's home had earned the official title of The Most Boring Place on Earth and Tiffany had keeled over from the lack of excitement.

If you can't beat 'em, join 'em. Holding her arms out to each side, Shayna flopped back like a rag doll. Why is it that nothing seemed to go as planned anymore?

Thank goodness the MBO picnic wasn't for another month. Not only would that give her enough time to live down the humiliation of their last meeting, it would give her time to regroup. The distance should help her clear Max out of her system once and for all. She'd focus all her energy on Jason McKnight, bachelor number three. No problem.

Shayna turned her head so she could meet Tiffany's eyes. A tiny smile curved the girl's cheeks as Shayna imitated her position. Shayna mentally ran down the list of activities she'd planned for the evening.

"Okay, Tif. Why don't we bake cookies to eat after lunch?"

"Nooo, it's too hot to bake."

"All right. Let's watch another video. I've got *Pocahontas*."

"Seen it already."

Shayna twisted her lips with growing frustration. "Do you want to do each other's hair and paint our toenails?"

"No."

"Watch TV?"

"No."

"Go to the movies?"

"Uh-uh."

"Play miniature golf?"

"Nope."

Shayna was at a loss and was about to suggest Tiffany take a nap, because she'd clearly gotten up on the wrong side of the bed, when the phone rang. Anxious for the sound of an adult voice, she leapt to her feet.

She picked up the phone in the kitchen. "Hello?"

"Hi, Shayna, it's Max."

At the sound of his voice, her heartbeat sped up. Her hand trembled slightly, and as she started to answer him, she accidentally pushed the receiver into her teeth. "Ouch!"

"Are you okay?"

"Yes, yes, I'm fine. What can I do for you?"

"Actually, I need a favor."

"Oh, Max, my niece is visiting this weekend, so I really can't—"

"It's not a big deal. I just need you to drop off the jacket I loaned you. I was planning to wear it to a meeting tomorrow."

"Oh! Of course! No problem!" She knew she was practically shouting, but she couldn't clear the image of Max showing up at his function the next day looking like he'd been mauled by a bear.

She'd taken the jacket back to the dry cleaner, and only a few of the red, strawberry filling stains had come out. Worse yet, as a last effort, she'd washed the jacket by hand and the delicate fabric had begun to fray in some areas.

"Do you mind dropping it off today?"

"Uh, not at all, but my niece and I have a few errands to run first. Are you going to be home?"

"Yeah, I'll be here all day."

"Okay then, I'll call when I'm on my way."

Shayna hung up the phone and stuck her head out of the kitchen door. "Problem solved, Tiffany. You and I are going to the mall."

"But I don't wa—"

"Yes you do, honey. This is an emergency."

Shayna stood outside Max's town house that evening, nervously clutching her new purchase. It had taken her four hours to find the right jacket. She and Tiffany had searched White Flint Mall, Lake Forest Mall and Montgomery Mall from top to bottom without any luck. Finally she found a store that carried the right jacket, but it had been the wrong color.

She forced the poor man in the store to call what seemed like every chain on the East Coast, searching for pearl gray. They'd finally found a jacket in Potomac Mills Mall in Virginia. After driving for an hour, Shayna discovered that the store only had two sizes left. Unwilling to take any chances, she'd bought both of them. Lord help her if neither one fit.

"Okay, Tif, wish me luck," she whispered just as the door opened.

"Well, hello, ladies. Come on in." He grinned at Shayna, then held his hand out to Tiffany. "You must be Shayna's niece."

Tiffany grasped his hand and shook it formally. "I'm Tiffany. Are you Aunt Shay's boyfriend?"

Max winked at Shayna, then gave Tiffany a big smile. "If that's your way of asking if I'm available, I'm all yours."

Tiffany giggled, instantly becoming shy.

Max stepped aside and pointed down the short set of stairs leading to his basement office. They could see a young boy sitting in front of Max's big-screen TV. "That's Kenny, my neighbor and part-time computer consultant. He's off the clock now. Kenny, put the game on pause and say hello to the ladies.''

''Can't,'' Kenny called without turning his head. ''I'm just about to destroy the mother ship.''

''I apologize for his rudeness, but Kenny takes saving the earth very seriously. A hero's work is never done.''

''That's okay. We understand. Here.'' Shayna thrust a jacket into Max's hands. She turned to Tiffany. ''Don't you want to watch Kenny save the earth?''

The little girl grinned. ''No, I'd rather watch this.'' Her eyes were bright with anticipation, as though an episode of ''Melrose Place'' was about to unfold right in front of her.

Max folded the jacket over his arm. ''Thanks for dropping this off.''

''Aren't you going to try it on?''

''What for?''

''Please. Just try it on.''

Looking both suspicious and intrigued, Max pulled the jacket off the hanger. ''What happened? Did you wash it and now you're afraid it may have shrunk?''

Shayna didn't answer. She and Tiffany watched as Max slipped his arm first through one sleeve and then the other. He straightened the lapels then held his arms out in front of him. Sure enough, the cuffs stopped midforearm.

Max grinned. ''Yep, I'd say it's just a bit…*tight.* But it's okay, Shayna. I don't—''

Sighing in resignation, Shayna turned to her niece.

"Okay, Tif, do me a favor and run out and get the other one."

"Sure, Aunt Shay." Tiffany headed for the door, muffling her giggles in the palm of her hand.

Max watched Tiffany go, looking perplexed. "*Other* one? What's going on?"

She bit her lip. "There was a bit of an accident."

He chuckled. "How come I'm not surprised?"

He reached up to fold his arms across his chest and Shayna became distracted by thin cloth stretching tight over Max's muscles like skin. What a fool she'd been to think that tiny jacket would fit. How could she have forgotten how broad and masculine his shoulders were? And his biceps... They bulged when he flexed, threatening to rip the material at the seams.

Shayna felt mesmerized by the well-cut outline of Max's torso. Oh, no, she mentally shook herself. So much for de-Maxing. Two minutes in his presence and she was already Maxed to the limit.

"Well, let me get out of this thing." He lifted his arms to peel off the jacket and they both froze at the unmistakable sound of material ripping. "Uh-oh."

Shayna shrugged in defeat as Tiffany returned. "Don't worry about it. There's more where that came from."

Tiffany came back carrying both the second jacket and the original jacket Shayna had ruined.

When Max finally managed to struggle out of the first one, Shayna thrust the second jacket into his hands.

"But, Shayna, you didn't have to—"

"Please, Max, just put it on."

With a sigh, Max pulled the jacket over his shoulders. This time the sleeves hung all the way down to his fingers. He waved his hand at her, watching the material flop up and down.

"Darn it. Now I have to return that one, too."

Max shrugged off the oversize jacket. "Really, Shayna, I wish you hadn't—wait a minute. There's another one?" He nodded to the final jacket in Tiffany's hands.

"That one is *your* jacket, Max. The one you originally loaned me. I can explain its condition—"

He took the jacket from Tiffany, staring at it as though he couldn't believe what he was seeing. Shayna could hear Tiffany's muffled giggles in the background, and hot embarrassment tinged her cheeks.

Max looked down at the stained and mangled material, shaking his head. Shayna held her breath when he finally lifted his gaze. Oh, no! There were tears in his eyes. His lips were parted as though he wanted to cry out, but no sound followed.

Shayna blinked, realizing that Max's chest was shaking, as he clutched the jacket in one hand and his stomach in the other. He gasped, releasing the thunder of laughter that had been trapped in his chest.

He took a deep breath, wiping the moisture from his eyes with the sleeve of the ragged jacket. "You had this at the bake sale, didn't you?"

Shayna nodded, still feeling wary. "I'd had it dry-cleaned for you."

"I think I remember seeing it," Max said, nearly choking on another round of laughter. "In fact, I think I may have wiped my face off on it."

He turned the jacket over. "Yeah, I think that's a chocolate impression of my nose right there."

"I'm sorry I ruined your jacket, Max. I tried to replace it and—"

"Shayna, listen to me. You didn't have to go to all that trouble. Why didn't you just tell me what had happened?"

"When dry cleaning didn't work, I thought I could clean it by hand, but the material started fraying, and then you called and said you needed it, and I thought I could find it at the mall and—"

"Breathe, girl, it's okay. I have a closet full of suits I don't wear. You didn't have to replace this one. I would have told you that if you'd talked to me first."

"No, Max, that isn't fair. I owe you a jacket, but since I couldn't find one—"

"I know… You found two. Why didn't you just ask the tailor to measure the first jacket to see if it would fit? I hate it that you wasted your money on this."

Shayna resisted the urge to smack her forehead. What was happening to her common sense? "Let me at least pay you what the jacket is worth."

"I won't take your money, Shayna."

"Then you replace the jacket and send me the bill, okay? I insist."

"Fine." He turned to Tiffany. "So, what do you ladies have planned for the rest of the evening?"

Tiffany shrugged. "Nothing."

"Tiffany, you know that's not true. We have lots of plans."

"Yeah, Aunt Shay, but all that stuff is boring."

Max quirked an eyebrow at Shayna, then grinned at Tiffany. "Oh, yeah? Well, Kenny and I were about to throw a couple of burgers on the grill. We'd be honored if you two would join us."

"I don't think so—" Shayna started, just as Tiffany piped up with "Cool! Can we, Aunt Shay?"

Shayna paused, turning in surprise to the little girl. "You want to stay?"

"Yes, please. Can't we?"

It would figure that the first activity her niece had shown interest in all day would be something that involved Max Winston—the one person on earth she wanted desperately to avoid.

"Come on, Shayna. Stay for dinner. Don't forget that, by your own admission, you owe me."

She looked from one expectant face to the other. She couldn't say no—certainly not after Tiffany had announced that all of Shayna's plans were "boring."

"All right, we can stay."

"Cool!" Tiffany bounded down the stairs to help Kenny save the earth, leaving Shayna with Max and three jackets.

Max took the jackets from her and tossed them on the couch. Shayna fought the instinct to cringe. She would have at least folded them first.

He crossed the living room and opened the sliding glass door that led to his deck. "Want to keep me company while I start the grill, or would you rather help the kids save the earth?"

Saving the earth would be safer, but she really didn't know much about video games.

"I can't remember the last time I barbecued," she said, following him out onto the deck. "I love the smell. It's one of those things that always remind you of summertime."

Max voiced his agreement, then retrieved barbecue fixings from the kitchen. Shayna watched as he juggled plates of hamburger patties, raw vegetables and buns. When he began balancing the plates precariously on the wooden banister of his deck, she had to speak up.

"You know...you can buy grill caddies to store your barbecue supplies and help you arrange your fixings. That way you wouldn't have to spread all your dishes on the rail and risk losing your meal to the grasshoppers."

Max just grinned and shrugged. "That's great, but this way has always worked just fine for me."

Shayna took a deep breath, folding her arms across her chest. "Okay." She paced up and down the deck. "It's a beautiful evening. Not too hot or too humid."

"Yeah." He nodded. "A pleasant break from the thick-air soup we've had lately."

Shayna cringed as he lifted the first round of patties onto a plate then wiped the greasy tongs off on his Chef's Do It With Relish apron.

"Here. Let me help you." She jumped up and began wiping off his grilling utensils with paper towels.

Max continued to cook.

Shayna returned to her perch on the other side of the deck, realizing that her helpful hints didn't seem to be sinking in. Max really was a great guy—not the guy for her, she reminded herself, but a great guy nonetheless. He would make some woman a wonderful catch with just a *tiny* bit of polishing.

An idea began to form in her head.

"Max, you don't plan to send me a bill for the jacket I ruined, do you?"

He turned away from the grill and wiped his hands off on his jeans—missing the apron completely.

Shayna gulped.

"I really don't need another jacket, Shayna. So there's no need to bill you."

"No, Max, I owe you. If you won't let me pay for the jacket, how about an exchange? I'll pay you back with my services instead."

His brow went up. "Hmm. That sounds interesting. Do these 'services' include you vacuuming my living room, wearing nothing but a frilly white apron?"

Shayna's body was instantly engulfed in heat. "No! Of course not. Get your mind out of the gutter." *And then pull mine out after it.*

She began pacing the deck, hoping to stir up enough of a breeze to cool her cheeks. "What I had in mind was more of a professional courtesy. I do consulting for a lot of MBO members. I thought I could give you a life management consultation. Just a couple of sessions."

"Really," Max said, grinning widely. "And what if I manage my life just fine on my own?"

She stopped cold. "Well, it was just a thought."

"I'm kidding, Shayna. That's a thoughtful offer. But I'd hate for you to waste your efforts. I'm a pretty hopeless case. I *like* my life the way it is."

Shayna's heart raced at the onset of an adrenaline rush. She felt a challenge coming on. "Yes, but how do you know you won't like it *better* once I've given you a management foundation that will help you organize your time more efficiently? You'll have more free time to do what you want."

"I already do what I want."

"Maybe, but how productive are you?"

Max laughed out loud. "You don't give up, do you? All right. What do I have to do?"

"Just sit down with me one afternoon and let me work up a plan. Then, based on that plan, I'll meet with you one or two more times to help you implement it. You'll be amazed."

He walked over to her. "I'm already amazed. Do you know that your entire face lights up when you talk about management foundations and implementing plans?" He cupped her cheek with his palm. "You're so beautiful."

Shayna's lips parted when his touch caught her off guard. She didn't move when his lips pressed into hers. His lower lip brushed her upper one, then he angled his head intensifying the kiss.

She opened for him, savoring his masculine taste with each deepening stroke.

"We did it! We won!" Shouts of victory penetrated her sensual fog.

Shayna jumped back from Max just before Tiffany and Kenny bounded out onto the deck. In her haste to get some distance from him, her elbow caught the edge of a plate balanced on the flat wooden railing.

The kids were dancing in circles, chanting, "We blew up the mother ship." And Max had already turned back to the grill, so no one noticed the fresh hot hamburgers go overboard.

"Uh, Max?" She tapped him on the back until he turned. "Were those the only burgers?"

"What? Why?"

Without turning to confirm the damage, Shayna pointed over her shoulder. Max leaned forward for a look. Shaking his head, he wiped his hands on his apron.

"I have more ground beef in the freezer." He looked over his shoulder at the kids. "Better find another planet to save, kids. Dinner's going to take a little longer than planned."

They ran off to play more video games, and Max headed to the kitchen, but he paused at the sliding glass door. "Okay, so maybe I *do* need to be a bit more organized but, sweetheart, steer clear of this next batch of burgers until I put one on your plate, okay?"

Shayna nodded sheepishly. With all the mishaps she'd been having lately, it was a wonder Max didn't declare her a local disaster area. Instead, he always made her smile.

Max defrosted the ground beef and whipped up a new batch of hamburgers in record time.

"Are you really going to eat all that?" Shayna asked, watching her niece pile onions, pickles, tomatoes and lettuce on her burger, which she customarily ate plain.

Shayna suspected Tiffany was trying to impress an older man. Kenny was eleven and he'd put two of everything possible on his burger. He'd tried to pile on two beef patties, but they wouldn't fit in his mouth so he had to settle for a burger in each fist.

"Yes, Aunt Shay. I love them this way." She slathered mustard on her bun, then tipped the jar toward Shayna. "Want some?"

"No." Shayna looked down at her modest burger with a leaf of lettuce and one slice of tomato. "Ketchup is enough for me."

She looked across the table to the ketchup bottle sitting next to Max's plate. He looked her directly in the eye and raised the bottle. "Is this what you want?" he asked slowly.

She bit her lip and nodded. He handed her the bottle, letting his fingers brush hers. She tugged on the bottle but he didn't release it right away. When she tugged harder, he grinned and let go.

"You sure you don't need help? It requires a lot of patience."

She twisted off the cap, shaking her head. "I'll be fine."

She turned the bottle over and gave it a good whack. Maybe working with Max was a bad idea.

Clearly he didn't know the difference between personal and professional behavior.

Whack!

She didn't need the hassle. No doubt he'd try to kiss her every chance he got.

Whack!

She wasn't interested in kisses. Well, she was interested, but not from—

Whack!

Suddenly the bottle slipped through her hands and exploded on the table. Ketchup and glass dumped onto her plate.

Kenny burst into laughter, Tiffany shrieked in horror and Max began fussing, cautioning everyone not to touch anything.

The girl pulled her ketchup-stained T-shirt away from her skin as though she were covered in blood. "Oh, no! Aunt Shay, you didn't send the chain letter, did you?"

7

Shayna stood in the middle of Max's office Monday afternoon. "Before we get started, Max, we need to get one thing straight."

He leaned back in his comfortable-looking leather chair, grinning mildly at her and clearly appreciating her figure. As soon as she'd walked into the house, he complimented her on her "lovely" dress. She'd been shooting for professional, but she hadn't realized how much the lavender silk conformed to her figure until it was too late.

"And which thing is that?" he asked, resting his chin on his palm as he studied her.

She began to pace the room, feeling self-conscious under his scrutiny. He obviously liked what he saw, and while, as a woman, she was flattered, she was really trying to do him a sincere favor and didn't want the distraction.

"This is a business meeting. Nothing else. Promise me you'll take that seriously."

He straightened in his chair and folded his arms over his chest. "Business meeting. Got it. But has anyone ever told you how shapely your legs are? And those high heels emphasize your sexy—"

"Max!" Shayna was tempted to turn around and run. Fighting him off was one thing, but it was becoming increasingly difficult to fight both Max and herself. "If you don't think you can—"

"Sorry. I'm just kidding, Shayna. This is a business meeting. I'll behave. Besides, I don't want to be accused of sexual harassment in the workplace." He motioned for her to continue.

She took a deep breath, trying to focus. This had been a bad idea, but it was too late to back out now. Out on the deck Saturday evening, she'd practically begged him to let her do this for him. Then he'd kissed her and all rational thought had disappeared.

Things had just gone downhill from there with the exploding ketchup bottle and Tiffany's mention of the chain letter. Fortunately, amidst the confusion of cleaning up the mess, no one seemed to register Tiffany's comment.

Maybe delving into the chaos that was Max's life would remind her why they wouldn't work as a couple in the first place. Avoiding him would only have made her attraction to him stronger. Giving herself a heavy dose of Max might be just what she needed to turn herself off him for good.

Her eyes strayed to his chiseled profile and the spark of mischief in his deep brown eyes. A girl can dream, can't she?

"Okay, back to business." She began pacing the room again, smoothing her palms against the sides of her dress. Why was she so nervous? This was her job. She did it every day, but showing off her professional skills to Max somehow seemed different.

"Since this is our first consultation, let me explain a little bit about how I work. Your life can be divided into three phases—your professional life, your social life and your personal life. My job is to help you balance these three phases so none of them are neglected."

Max rubbed his chin, seeming to consider her words carefully. "That's very interesting, Shayna. I'm curious. What do you do to keep a well-balanced social life?"

Shayna tensed, then forced herself to relax. New clients often asked about her personal experiences with these life management theories. His question wasn't so unusual, as long as she answered it professionally.

"Actually, balance doesn't always mean giving each phase equal time within the same day. Sometimes you need to focus on one phase for a period of time and then you can make up for it later. While I was setting up my business, I had to devote a bigger chunk of time to my professional phase. Now I balance the time I devoted in that area by allowing myself more of the social and personal phases."

"I see, and do you think that you can—"

"I'll be happy to answer your questions later, but first I need you to write down three goals for each of these phases. Then we'll begin to work up a plan around them."

Shrugging, Max took out a legal pad and began jotting down his goals. He was finished in less than a minute.

Shayna frowned at him. "Max, take your time. This is important."

"I'm a simple man, Shayna. My goals are simple."

"Okay. Read them aloud."

He lifted the pad. "Professional phase. I want to continue making a living wage, I want to continue producing a high-quality newsletter with up-to-date gaming tips, I want to continue to be my own boss and make my own decisions."

"Those are very good, but you should also think about the long term. Don't you want to expand or increase your—"

"Nope. These *are* my long-term goals."

Shayna was surprised by his utter lack of ambition. What a waste of such obvious talents. He could be and do so much, and he seemed to be limiting himself. She shook her head in frustration. "Go on. What are the rest?"

"Social phase. I want to volunteer more for MBO, I want to be a better neighbor, I want to make love to Shayna Gunther."

She caught her breath. Her gaze darted to his so she could reprimand him for his little joke. But when their eyes met, she saw that he was quite serious.

Swallowing hard, Shayna shifted her weight to the arm that was resting on the corner of his desk, and lost her balance. She almost toppled back into a rack of video game cartridges that was stacked behind her. Luckily she caught herself just in time.

"Are you okay?"

"Yes, yes, I'm fine."

He continued to read from the pad as though nothing had happened. "Personal phase. I want to be happy, I want to be healthy, I want to have fun."

"Hmm. Uh, very good. You're right. You do have very simple goals."

"I told you that I would be wasting your efforts, Shayna. Most of my goals I've already satisfied. But there is that one you can help me with...."

Shayna chose to ignore him. Yet his words still echoed in her mind. He wanted to make love to her. A thrill raced down her spine. This was a bad idea. A very bad idea. It had been a long time for her, and just the thought of—

She clutched her arms, trying to hide the goose bumps raising on them. "The next thing we need to do is figure out how to restructure things to better facilitate some of these goals. Time management is one of the most basic steps. Many goals aren't reached because people don't feel they have ample time to pursue them. One technique is to combine energies. While you're doing the laundry, you can dictate a correspondence into a tape recorder and start preparing dinner."

She continued her lecture, unsure how much of it Max was really absorbing. "Okay, now let's examine your typical day and see where we can make changes."

"That's just it, Shayna. I don't have a 'typical' day, and I like it that way. I don't do schedules and routines anymore."

She felt her frustration growing. Couldn't he see that she was trying to help him? "It's not a routine so much as a guideline for your time. For instance, when you wake up in the morning, do you—"

He held up a hand. "Hold on. You're asking for a lot here, Shayna. Why should I turn my life upside down, rearranging things, when I'm perfectly happy with the way things are? Why should I change my life-style just because you think there's something wrong with it?"

"I'm not saying there's anything wrong. I'm just pointing out that there's always room for improvement. Ways to do things more efficiently. Please just hear me out and you'll see the advantages as we go along."

Finally he shrugged. "Okay, continue." He crossed his arms over his chest and watched her patiently.

Shayna took a deep breath, feeling the pressure in her chest mount. Max really wasn't cooperating. He was normally such a laid-back, easygoing man. Why did he have to make waves now?

Focus, Shayna. This will work out. "Let's start with your desk. I see you don't have In and Out bins. I also keep a file holder on my desktop to help me prioritize my mail. Prioritization is a key in time management."

Max surprised her by nodding his head. "You know, when I worked for Windgate Software, I had a co-worker, Walker Hines, who operated on that same principle.''

She raised her brows. ''Oh, see… Good advice is universal.'' She began sorting through the items on his desk, stacking paperwork to one side. ''One organization principle that really seems to help is color coordination—red for urgent, yellow for high priority, blue for low priority. The code can follow through with tabs, rubber bands, paper clips, Post-it notes—''

''I believe Hines used to use color-coded file folders. I remember him mentioning that more and more work was ending up in the 'urgent' folder.''

Shayna nodded. ''Well, there you go.'' She smiled to herself. It seemed that she was finally beginning to get through to him. He was listening to her ideas and actually making associations. Whoever this Hines person was, Max seemed to respect him. He was ready for the big guns.

''Now let's talk about scheduling. I've noticed that you don't wear a watch.'' She turned around in the room. ''I don't see a clock anywhere. The only way you can manage your time is to keep track of it.''

He shook his head. ''I like to keep my own pace. I have a stereo in my bedroom with a clock, my VCR has one and so does the radio in my car. That's enough for me.''

''Max, you'd be surprised how much you can get done in a day by planning your time. Calendars and daily planners are just the beginning. I have a watch with an alarm that allows me to spend a set amount of time on each task. That way—''

Max rubbed his chin. "I remember Hines having a watch like that. It seemed the alarm was always going off and he was rushing from one place to the next. He didn't have time for actual calendars. He used a computerized organizer that fit in the palm of his hand. He walked around with a computer printout of his schedule, with dates and times highlighted and notes crammed into the margins. It was nothing less than amazing what he could accomplish in a day's time."

Shayna put her hands on her hips. "Well, Max, you seem to really admire this Hines guy. He seems to have a really well-organized routine. Since you seem to respect him, why don't you want to be more like him?"

Max took a moment to consider her question. "I did," he said quietly. "In fact, I wanted to *be* him. We were the same age, but he was my mentor. At thirty-two, Hines was the youngest Windgate employee to be made executive in charge of development. The virtual reality game he designed was the top seller that year. I wanted to walk in his footsteps."

"There's nothing wrong with that. What happened?"

"His footsteps led to an open grave. Hines died of a massive heart attack two years ago."

Shayna gasped, stunned into immobility. "Oh, my…I—I'm sorry."

"I had one foot in after him, Shayna. We were so much alike, we could have been brothers. We ate lunch at the same fast-food joints. Kept the same sixty-hour work schedules. Had the same hunger and drive to get ahead, no matter what it took.''

Shayna's heart was racing. She stumbled backward until she found herself sitting down. It didn't faze her in the least that she was sitting on a coffee table top.

"The only difference between us was that Hines died suddenly, leaving behind a young bride and a three-month-old baby. His heart attack was a wake-up call that I took very seriously, Shayna. Walker Hines will never get a second chance.''

Max took advantage of her silence, moving to kneel before her.

"Obsessive schedules, pressing deadlines, back-breaking routines all add stress to the body, Shayna. I'm not in the business of stress anymore, but it seems that you are.''

She flinched.

"All I'm saying is that life should be savored, sipped slowly like fine brandy. What's the use of making yourself sick with insane schedules and routines if you never get to relax and have a little fun?''

Shayna stood and retrieved her purse. "You were right. This was a mistake. I'm sorry I wasted both our time.''

"Shayna, wait.''

She slipped away from his grasping fingers, ran up the basement stairs and slammed the door behind her.

"That's a very intriguing goal, Gloria, but remember, we're trying to keep things in perspective,''

Shayna told her sixty-three-year-old client Tuesday afternoon. "I don't think the D.C. government would appreciate you skinny-dipping in the reflecting pool."

"This is probably true," Gloria said, running her hand through her shocking red spiky hair. "But it's something I want to do before I die. Don't forget that I did accomplish all of last month's goals. Which includes seeing my artwork displayed for public enjoyment."

"You're right. A good reminder not to underestimate yourself." Shayna chose not to mention that the police mistook the "artwork" she'd displayed in a national park for graffiti and that her husband had paid a hefty fine to have it removed.

"And I gotta thank you, Shayna. My hubby probably woulda left me by now if you hadn't helped me pull it together."

Shayna squeezed her hand, acknowledging Gloria's gratitude and wishing Max could be there to witness it. Her schedules and routines *did* help people. So what if yesterday he'd practically accused her of being in the business of inducing heart attacks. Gloria Diamonte was *living* proof that her life management consultations could work.

She studied the older woman who wore shiny black leggings, a full face of bright makeup and a T-shirt sporting a homemade collage that could have been assembled in a junkyard.

Six months ago, Gloria had been a hopeless slob, leaving trails of clothing, candy wrappers and cigarette butts wherever she went. She'd just married a

wealthy man half her age who'd had no idea Gloria
had such poor grooming habits. He'd brought in maid
after maid, all of whom couldn't take more than a
month of Gloria's slovenliness. Finally, after Gloria
scared off the fifth housekeeper and nearly burned
down the house with her haphazardly strewn cigarette
ashes, Frank Diamonte had had enough. Shayna, life
management consultant and miracle worker, had been
their last hope.

Shayna's gaze zeroed in on a shiny piece of tin
reflecting off Gloria's T-shirt. *Unconventional* didn't
begin to describe the flighty, abstractly artistic older
woman across from her. There had been nothing she
could do about Gloria's horrible, clashing taste in
clothing. Or music, she thought, once again tuning out
the bizarre cross between druid chants and heavy
metal playing in the background. But week after
week, Shayna introduced order into the woman's life
in small doses.

Gloria caught the direction of her gaze. "You like
my T-shirt? I could do you one."

Shayna bit her lip, taking in the bolts, screws,
rocks, chunks of colored plastic and what looked like
little bits of tire rubber covering the shirt. "Oh, I
couldn't ask you to do that."

Unsnapping a long glittery change purse, Gloria
pulled out a cigarette. "Ask shmask, I'm offerin'."

"In that case, thank you." Shayna still hadn't figured out what to do with the life-size portrait Gloria
had given to her three months into their consultations.
It was an abstract made entirely out of beans. Right

now it was stored in the back of her pantry. She figured if her business ever had a bad year, she had an emergency stash of beans to see her through.

She didn't know what Frank Diamonte, a conservative investment broker in his mid-thirties saw in Gloria. But she did know one thing: he had great taste. Working with Gloria for the last six months had been both a pleasure and an adventure. And she was glad she'd been able to help.

While Gloria got up to put a new CD in the compact disc changer, Shayna studied her hands. This is what life management consulting was all about. Max had missed the point entirely.

The more she thought about it, the more clear it became in her mind. She understood Max's fear now. But he was avoiding order and organization for all the wrong reasons. The schedules or the routines had not given his friend a heart attack, it was the lack of balance.

If she'd known what Max's fears were, going in, she would have taken an entirely different approach. They wouldn't focus on the business aspect of life management. The foundation she'd proposed to him covered all areas of living. He needed to organize his kitchen, and she hadn't seen his closet, but if it were anything like his silverware drawer...

Yesterday, when Max had told her about Walker Hines, she'd felt hurt and even angry for the way he'd presented the story to her. Now she was realizing that she couldn't let her anger get in the way of helping

Max. He needed to see that organization was nothing to be afraid of.

Max watched in a daze as the enemy planes swooped out of the clouds and blew up his last fighter pilot. The screen exploded in a ball of flames. He'd blown it.

He was trying to break in a new video game, but his concentration was shot, and he kept getting killed within the first few screens. The scene that had sent Shayna storming out of his house yesterday kept replaying in his mind. This time, he'd blown it with her for good.

He'd come on too strong. Instead of making a point, he'd practically accused her of causing heart attacks. Heart palpitations maybe, but he hadn't meant to come down so hard on her.

Max had only wanted to make her see that there was more to life than schedules and routines. Time management and order weren't her only choices.

It would have been one thing if she were thriving on it, but clearly it was getting to her. She had a short attention span, she dropped things and became quickly flustered. It had to be the stress of these schedules she insisted on keeping.

He couldn't stand by and watch Shayna make herself a slave to the frenzy of her rigid life-style, but he doubted she'd ever speak to him again.

The phone rang and Max flipped screens to check his computerized caller ID system. The number he saw nearly made his heart stop. He grabbed the receiver. "Shayna?"

"I…uh, how did you know it was me?"

"Caller ID."

"Oh. I'm calling to schedule our next consultation."

Max nearly swallowed the gum he was chewing. "Our next consultation?"

"You're not ready to give up, are you? After our last meeting, I've decided to take a different approach. Max, you don't have to be afraid of ending up like Hines. Life management consulting will help you find balance. Will you let me help you?"

His brow wrinkled. She made him sound like a candidate for rehab. "I wanted to apologize for the way our last session turned out. I didn't mean to imply that—"

"Believe me, Max, I understand. And now that I understand, I think I know how to help you. How about Thursday? Are you free?"

"Yes, but—"

"Great. Two o'clock?"

"Sure, but—"

"Perfect. I'll see you then." She hung up.

Max stared at the phone, wondering what Shayna had in mind for him. She seemed determined, and she was definitely on a mission.

He grinned, hanging up the phone. That was okay. He had a mission, too. So she was redoubling her efforts to organize his life, was she? All right, a little organizing wouldn't hurt. And in the meantime, he would redouble his efforts to schedule a little relaxation and fun into Shayna's routine.

He rubbed his hands together in anticipation. Seduction had just leapt to the top of the list of activities he was going to incorporate into Shayna's life.

———◆———

8

"Ohh, Max! Ohh, Max, no!"

"Yes, Shayna. I warned you that it would be like this."

"But it's so...ohh my goodness."

"You said you were ready for it. You said this was what you wanted to do."

"You're right. I wasn't ready for this," she said, peering into Max's walk-in closet. What looked like hundreds of shoes covered the floor; shirts and pants were slipping off hangers; and sweater sleeves and corners of T-shirts were dripping like icicles from the wall-mounted shelves.

Max laughed. "I know this must be closet hell for you. It's not too late to back out. We can close the door and you can pretend it was all just a terrible nightmare."

Shayna ignored him. "What are those mounds on the floor over there?"

"My dirty laundry."

"Haven't you ever heard of a hamper?"

"A what?"

"A hamper."

"A what?"

"A ham—" She punched him in the arm. "Stop acting silly. Where do you keep your dirty clothes?"

"I thought it was obvious. I keep them in mounds on the floor in the back of my closet." He laughed. "Haven't you heard that joke? How do men sort their laundry? Filthy, and filthy but wearable."

Shayna laughed. "How true. But we're going to work on that." She looked up and spotted a laundry basket on the shelf above her. "Why don't you use that—wait, what have you got in there?"

She pulled it down, then turned to him in dismay. "You keep supplies for your fish tank in your laundry basket?"

Max held his hand to his forehead in feigned despair. "What can I tell you? After Pepe died, I couldn't face the empty tank, so I gave it to Kenny. He didn't want the extra gravel, and he already had a water filter. I had to put them somewhere...."

Shaking her head, Shayna walked over to Max's nightstand and scribbled on a sheet of paper. She ripped it off the pad and handed it to him. "This is the most important piece of information I give my clients."

He stared blankly at the paper. "What is it?"

"The number to Goodwill."

"Thanks." With a grin Max shoved it into the back pocket of his jeans.

Shayna scanned his bedroom, taking in the dark masculine colors of navy blue and gray. A touch of forest green would really waken the room up, she thought, making a mental note. The wall across from the bed had a built-in shelving unit that housed several rows of books, a television, stereo, VCR and, of course, a video game entertainment center. He had a small desk against the windows and night tables on either side of the bed.

She let her gaze roll over to Max's king-size bed. The sheets were pulled up to meet the pillows but they were rumpled.

"Don't you believe in making your bed?"

Max frowned. "What is this 'bed making' you speak of? Some kind of craft? I lead a full life. I don't have time for new hobbies."

She resisted the smile she felt curving at her cheeks. "Never mind."

Shayna walked to the entrance of his closet and looked over her shoulder. "Are you ready to tackle this? We have our work cut out for us. The shoes alone. They say women buy a lot of shoes. How many sneakers does one man need?"

"I'm an athletic guy," he said, flexing his shoulders. "I need basketball shoes, and running shoes, and I can't wear running shoes to play tennis. Every guy has got to have a basic high-top, classic fish heads, Chuck Taylor and Converse All-Star shoes. Then, of course, you've got to have a pair of Nike, Air Jordan and—"

"Okay, okay," Shayna said, raising both arms in surrender. "I'm sorry I asked. Anyway, are you ready to get to work?"

"In a minute. I think you'd better let me kiss you

first. That way when I'm cooped up in that cramped little space with you, I can keep my mind on straightening instead of daydreaming about the feel of your lips.''

Shayna held up her hands to ward him off. ''Oh, no. We're not playing any of your cute little games. When I got here, you promised to behave, and I'm going to hold you to that.''

''I'd rather have you hold me to *you*. Besides, you never defined the word *behave*. What ain't misbehaving to me might be downright naughty to you.''

''Max, we're not having this conversation. Just get to work.''

''One more thing.''

''What?'' she said in exasperation.

''I can't work without music.''

What a surprise. Gloria Diamonte had said the same thing when the time came to tackle her attic full of junk. Somehow Shayna had survived the new age heavy metal druid music, so she knew she could handle whatever Max had in mind.

''What's it going to be?'' she asked. ''Golden oldie Motown hits?''

''No, that's driving music,'' he said, walking over to the stereo. ''We need cleaning-out-the-closet music.''

''Oh? And what would that be?''

''You'll see. Go ahead and get started. I'll join you in a minute.''

Shayna made a spot for herself in the middle of Max's closet floor. She felt like she'd invented a new matching game. She'd pick up one of Max's sneakers, hunt through the pile until she found its mate and then arrange the pair neatly against the wall.

A few minutes later a spicy salsa rhythm filled the room. Max appeared in the doorway, swiveling his hips to the Latin tempo. "Whenever I hear this music, I just have to dance."

Shayna turned her attention back to the shoes, trying to block out the image of Max's sensual undulations. "Well, you're supposed to be cleaning, so put on some music that gets you in the mood for that."

"It's too late, the beat is in my blood now. Do you salsa?"

She begged her eyes not to look up, but they betrayed her. She had to hand it to him, he wasn't bad. His dancing was much better than his singing. "Only with chips."

He held a hand out to her as he continued to gyrate. "Come here. I'll show you how."

"No, Max, stop goofing off. Come in here and help me."

"Okay." Max danced his way into the closet and picked up a shoe in each hand. Then he began dancing around her in the little circle she'd cleared for herself, waving the shoes and clapping them together as he moved.

Shayna sighed in frustration. "Max!"

"If you can't beat 'em, join 'em, sweetheart. How can you tell me this music isn't getting to you? How do you know you won't like it, if you don't try it?"

He reached down and dragged Shayna to her feet.

"What are you doing?"

He grabbed her hands. "Don't you feel it? Come on. Dance with me." He rocked her back and then began dancing her forward out of the closet.

She tried to hold her body stiff, resisting him and the music, but it was impossible to ignore the Latin rhythm pulsing through the air. It really was enticing. Max rotated his hips, stepping forward and back, twirling her around his arm, pulling her close and dipping her low.

The music was so lively and the chorus of singers seemed to be having so much fun, that Shayna found herself enjoying herself. Before she knew it, they were doing salsa steps all around his bedroom. He stood her up on a chair and clapped his hands around her while she shimmied and posed. Then he lifted her off and danced her around the bed again.

The music reached a crescendo, and Max leapt up onto the bed for a solo number, then he reached down to pull her up after him. She was unprepared for the unevenness of the mattress and her feet immediately became entangled with his.

They both went down, landing on the bed with a huge bounce. A wave of giggles erupted from Shayna's lips as she tried to calm her heavy breathing. "Wow. That was fun."

Max was above her, and when she raised her gaze, she expected to see the same lighthearted mood she felt reflected in his eyes. Instead, the serious set of his countenance made her breath catch in her throat.

His eyes were locked on hers. She almost looked away from their intensity.

The music on the stereo was now a slow sultry Latin song that fit the sudden change in mood. She felt Max's hand at her waist. His gaze never broke from hers as his head lowered.

This kiss was very different from the teasing sensual kisses they'd shared before. His lips remained closed as they brushed over hers, but the shifting of his hand at her waist, gently pressing her into him, magnified the desire building within her.

She found herself cupping his face in her hands. A tiny moan escaped her lips as she twisted restlessly beneath him, opening her mouth under his. She licked at his closed lips until he allowed her inside.

"Shayna." He groaned her name, before deepening the kiss. He let the hand at her waist slowly glide up her torso until his palm cupped her breast. His thumb played with the nipple through her blouse until the bud went rigid.

He pressed a knee between her legs, and she arched against him, bringing their bodies to full contact. He leaned into her, dragging his mouth away from hers to find the tender skin just beneath her jaw. He nibbled and licked, until she arched up against him again.

"That's it, baby. I want you so much." His left hand raked back her hair as he brought his mouth down on hers once again.

She dipped her arms under his so she could wrap her arms around his back. Her hands ran over the rough denim of his jeans, then slid upward, tugging his T-shirt from the waistband. She wanted to feel skin.

Shayna's thoughtful meticulous brain had shut down at the first brush of his lips. The sensation of being close to Max, and the desire to be closer, were her only thoughts now.

The first touch of her fingertips on the smooth skin of his muscled back caused his body to bow, sinking his arousal into her, pressing their bodies tighter together.

Her palms grazed the muscles of his back as she caressed upward, and her nails skimmed the trench of his spine on the down stroke.

Max's tongue dipped into her mouth again and again as his hands moved restlessly over her clothes. "Please. I want to make love to you, Shayna."

Those words echoed in her head, slowly bringing her away from what Max was doing to her body. Her mind replayed those words, not as he'd just said them, but as she'd heard them on Max's list of social goals.

She was a goal he wanted to accomplish. Not a person, but an achievement. As her mind became more alert, she realized she was no better. She'd made a list of eligible bachelors and had pursued them, not as people but as goals.

Shayna's mind was racing now. Max's hands had moved to the buttons of her blouse and she stopped him with a hand over his.

"I can't do this, Max." She slid from beneath him and sat on the edge of the bed with her back to him. She felt his weight shift on the bed and assumed he was sitting up, as well. "Shayna? What's wrong, honey? I thought you—"

"Really, I just can't. It's not right." She stood. "I'd better go."

"No, wait. I'm not going to let you run out on me again. If you don't want me to touch you anymore, it's okay. I give you my word that I won't, but please, talk to me."

She sank back down on the bed, but didn't turn to face him. She couldn't tell him about the eligible bachelors list. Especially now that she'd realized how silly the whole idea had been. Her feelings for Max proved that the perfect mate couldn't be picked intellectually, based on a list of required characteristics.

Suddenly she didn't care about ambitious men with conservative haircuts and six-figure incomes. Max wasn't good for her. He made her life crazy and chaotic, and yet she wanted him anyway.

It was all so mixed-up; she didn't want to make a mistake, making her already-confused life worse. "I don't know what to say to you, Max. If you want me to stay, let's get back to straightening out your closet, but I can't offer you anything more than that right now."

"Then I'll just have to be satisfied with that."

They returned to the closet, working side by side in near-perfect silence. As they cleaned, Shayna cataloged all the reasons why she and Max could never be happy together.

For starters, his closet was a disaster area.

He was unfamiliar with the concept of making a bed.

He considered plastic all-star basketball dishes fine china.

Shayna tried to continue from there, but she kept running into arguments that worked against the case she was trying to make.

Things like, he thought her mishaps were cute or endearing instead of embarrassing and clumsy.

And he could cook like a dream.

Not to mention his kisses were better than a triple chocolate sundae dripping with hot fudge.

With Max just a few feet away, Shayna decided to give up her thoughts entirely and focus on cleaning the closet.

When they were through, Max's shoes were lined up in neat rows against one wall. His shirts and pants—which Shayna insisted on arranging according to color, though he protested they wouldn't last a day that way—were hanging straight and crisp. His sweaters and T-shirts were folded on the top shelf, his dirty laundry was sorted into the laundry basket and he had a full box of items for Shayna to drop off at Goodwill.

Max walked Shayna out to her car. "So when is our next consultation?"

Shayna mentally reviewed her calendar. "How about Saturday?" When he agreed, she said, "I think it will be our last."

Max nodded slowly. "Then we'll have to make it count."

9

"Shayna, something has come up," Max said, when he opened the door for her, Saturday afternoon.

Shayna stepped into the foyer and, without missing a beat, pulled out her daily planner. "No problem. When do you want to reschedule?"

"No." He reached over and snapped the planner closed. "That won't be necessary. I just need to drop a box of newsletters off with a client. Then we can go on with whatever you have planned."

"Okay." Shayna smiled politely, and Max grinned back, his face showing relief. She crossed to his living room and sat down. Opening her briefcase, she began sorting through papers.

She glanced around, taking in the two-foot tower of magazines stacked haphazardly by his well-worn recliner. Mentally she organized the magazines into a rack, arranged alphabetically.

There was still so much she could do for him, but this had to be their last session. Her feelings for Max were stronger than she'd realized, and that could only mean trouble. When he was near, she lost her balance and her ability to focus.

"What are you doing?"

She looked over at Max guiltily, knowing he couldn't possibly have read her thoughts. "I thought I could get some of my own work done while you run your errand."

"You're going to wait here?" His tone was surprised.

"Sure." She pulled three colored pens from her briefcase to make notes in her date book. "You don't mind, do you?"

"Well, I thought you could come with me. I won't be long."

She looked back down at the work on her lap, taking the cap off her purple pen. "Really, I don't mind waiting here."

Max began pacing. "What did you have planned for today?"

"Actually, since this will be our last consultation, I thought we could go over some organization tips and tricks. I usually leave my clients with some hints to help them manage on their own."

"Perfect. We can go over those in the car." He walked over, helped her up and prodded her out the front door before she could protest further.

Once in his truck, Shayna pulled a clipboard out of her briefcase. She glanced out the window as he pulled onto the highway. "Where exactly is this client you need to see?"

"College Park, near the University of Maryland," Max said vaguely.

She returned her attention to her clipboard. "Now

I have a checklist of ten items for us to go over. Reminders to help you organize your time.''

"Just ten items, huh?"

She raised her brows at him. "You sound disappointed."

"No, just surprised."

"Well, trust me. The list is complete."

"Okay, let'er rip."

"Number one. Set goals. We've already had extensive discussion on this topic, so we can move on to item number two."

She didn't want to remember the third item on his list of social goals, but, lately, it was all she *could* think about. Shayna retreated behind her mask of professionalism. Maintaining a crisp formal tone, she quickly knocked out the first five items on the list. "Number six—"

"Hold on. What was item number four again?"

"Using to-do lists."

"I have a question about that."

"Yes?"

"Um…is there…uh, a limit to the number of items you can include on a to-do list?"

"No, but you don't want the list to become so long and overwhelming that you feel you'll never accomplish all your goals. Then it becomes self-defeating. It's best to keep it short. Once the first list is finished, you can make a new one. Plus, you'll experience a real sense of accomplishment. Does that answer your question?"

Max nodded.

"Okay. Number six—"

"Wait. I have another question."

She sighed. "Yes?"

This was the most interest he'd shown since they'd begun working together. If she didn't know better, she'd think he was stalling.

"Do you think it's ever too late to teach an old dog new tricks?"

"What?"

"Do you think a person can ever be too old to change?"

"No, it's never too late to make a positive change in your life."

"So you think it's possible for someone to adopt new habits even though it may go against their nature?"

"Yes. Of course. No one has all the answers. Most of us do change our life-styles as we grow older. We reevaluate what we want from life, and begin pursuing other avenues." She became quiet for a minute, turning those words around in her mind.

"Sometimes plans that seemed like perfectly good ideas at the time of their conception, later seem silly and frivolous." Her eligible bachelors list suddenly flashed in her mind.

"We realize that some things in life just can't be planned for," she said more slowly. "We have to be flexible and realize when it's time to stop fighting..."

She felt Max steal a glance at her profile. Could he tell that she was no longer talking about him? She felt her cheeks heat at the intensity of her emotions.

After a minute she raised her clipboard again. "Okay, item number six—"

"We're here, Shayna."

"We're where?" She looked around the shopping center.

He parked the car and opened the door. "Come on."

"Shouldn't I wait here?"

"No. Sunny can get really chatty sometimes. With you around, he might resist the urge. He's kind of shy." He grabbed his box of newsletters and crossed the parking lot with Shayna trailing behind him.

When he stopped to pull open the door, she paused to read the sign. "Duckpin bowling?"

"Yeah. Every bowling alley has an arcade, and my newsletters sell like hotcakes because a lot of the college kids hang out here."

Shayna followed him down the stairs, scrunching up her nose at the musty smell. She felt like she was walking into someone's basement. "What *is* duckpin bowling? And don't tell me it involves hurling balls at our fine-feathered friends."

"No, it just means the ball and pins are smaller than regular tenpin bowling, and the rules are a little different."

"How come I've never heard of this game before?" she asked, watching the two busy lanes at the end where the league bowlers wore lime green polyester shirts with White Oak Duckpin Bowling embroidered on them.

"You should have. The sport was invented in Baltimore, Maryland." He led her over to the counter.

"Hey, Max, my man. What's up?" All this was said in a surprisingly monotone voice, his expression never changing.

Shayna assumed this was Sunny. For a man with such a bright name, he had an ironically dark and brooding look about him, with his Native American features, straight black hair and hooded eyes.

"Sunny, how's life, buddy?" Max set his box of newsletters on the countertop.

"Business is pretty slow right now. Thanks for dropping off a new supply. Last night a busload of high school kids touring the university bought out my supply. The video game junkies have already started trickling in this afternoon looking for your newsletter."

"No problem. I'm just glad they're still in demand." He looked over his shoulder at Shayna. "This is my—" he grinned "—life management consultant, Shayna Gunther."

Shayna held out her hand to the man. "How do you do?"

Sunny squeezed her fingers, squinting at her. "Life management what?"

She reached into her purse and pulled out her business card. "Max was referring to my career. Life management consulting. I help my clients become more organized."

Sunny stared at the card, nodding slowly. He turned toward Max. "Hey, man, thanks for making a special trip out here. The lanes don't usually fill up until later in the evening. Why don't you and the lady stay and play a couple of games on the house?''

"We'd like that."

"We can't."

Max and Shayna spoke at the same time, leaving Sunny to glance back and forth between them looking puzzled.

"Give us a second, Sunny." Max took Shayna's elbow and pulled her aside. "Shayna, I know we have a schedule to keep, but I've been doing business with Sunny for a couple years now, and he's never offered me anything for free. He might be offended if we don't take advantage of his hospitality."

Shayna glanced back at Sunny. He did look like the type of guy she wouldn't want to offend. "But, Max, I don't even know how to play."

"I've never actually played, either, but I'm sure we can figure it out. Just one game. Please?"

Finally she shrugged. Why not? She wasn't as inflexible as Max made her out to be. "Okay, just one game. Do we have to wear bowling shoes?''

"Yeah." Max walked over to Sunny. "We're all set."

Sunny set them up with bowling shoes and a score sheet and sent them over to the center lane. Great, Shayna thought to herself, now everyone who walked in could get the best view of her humiliating herself.

Max laid the score sheet on the table and wrote both their names on it. "Now, all I know is that in duckpin bowling we play three frames per round instead of two.''

Shayna, who was perched on the end of her chair, trying not to think about how many people had worn these shoes before her, frowned. ''What does that mean?''

''It means you have three chances to knock down all the pins instead of just two.''

''Oh, okay. I've never played duckpins before, but I'm not a bad tenpin bowler.''

Adjusting to the smaller ball took some time, and Shayna rolled gutter balls the first few frames. But she did eventually get a feel for the game, rolling several strikes that evened the score between the two of them.

While Shayna took her next turn, Max went over to the jukebox and played what he couldn't know was one of her personal favorites of all the Motown hits, ''I Can't Help Myself'' by the Four Tops.

Of course he insisted on singing along, loud and off-key as he'd been known to do. Strangely enough, Shayna didn't mind his bad singing. Instead, she got caught up in the rich timbre of his voice. He knew all the words and sang them with gusto. When he got to the chorus describing a guy loving a girl it was easy to imagine him directing those words toward her.

She looked over her shoulder and almost dropped the small but heavy ball on her foot. Max was standing behind her, imitating the classic moves of the Four Tops, shuffling from side to side and spinning.

Shaking her head, Shayna refused to let him distract her from her game. She approached the line, and as she pulled back her arm, her right foot crossed a little too far behind her left and she knocked herself in the ankle as she released the ball.

The ball stuttered down the lane, then veered into the gutter.

Hopping on one foot, she moved toward Max. "That was all your fault!"

He shrugged innocently.

Shayna choked on her last round and rolled three frames of gutter balls.

Max took his last turn and won the game by fifteen points. "Maybe we should have taken one of the bumper lanes. At least that way you couldn't get any gutter balls."

"Very funny. It just takes a while to get the hang of the game. Besides, I don't think you're playing fair, distracting me with your caterwauling. I can redeem myself if we play one more game."

Max shrugged and set up the score sheet for another round. As Shayna approached the line to take her turn, Max called out to her. "You know what I think your problem is? You're not putting enough weight behind the ball. These balls aren't as heavy as regular bowling balls. Just aim for the center and give it a little force."

Max's advice made Shayna self-conscious. When she tried to release the ball, she froze. "I don't think I understand what you mean."

"Here," Max said. "Let me show you."

He came up behind her and showed her how to aim

the ball by wrapping his arms around hers and swinging her arm to and fro. Shayna could smell his masculine cologne, and as he moved her arm, his muscled chest pressed against her back. Finally he stepped back from her. "Okay, now let go just the way I showed you."

Still distracted by Max's nearness, Shayna found it hard to concentrate. What had he instructed her to do? Oh, yeah, put some force behind the ball. Deciding to go for broke, she swung her arm back and threw the ball down the lane.

The ball hurtled down the lane arcing upward, until a thunderous boom, much like a gunshot echoed through the bowling alley.

She clapped her hands over her ears and hit the floor. "Oh my goodness! Is someone shooting at us?"

Max came forward and pulled her to her feet. "No, Shayna, look." He pointed down the lane.

Her eyes widened. Glass covered the lower portion of the lane. "Where did all that glass come from?"

He grinned, shaking his head. "Your ball. You threw it too high. It hit one of the fluorescent lights in the ceiling."

She stared at him incredulously. "You're kidding me."

He shook his head. "Nope."

Instantly Sunny was behind them.

"Oh, no! Sunny, I'm so sorry."

He had a broom and dustpan in hand. "Don't worry, Shayna. You're not the first person to do this. It happens." Sunny made his way down the lane and swept up the broken glass. "You can finish your game now."

Shayna looked at Max. "Your bowl."

He turned his back to pick up the score sheet. "No, you have two more frames in your turn. Go for it."

At this point, she was ready to go home, but she didn't want Max to think she was a quitter. Still, she wanted the game to be over as soon as possible. Picking up two balls, she rolled them down the lane, one right after the other.

The balls had already begun their journey by the time she saw the man lowering himself from a hole in the ceiling above the duckpins. She covered her face in horror. "Oh, no! What is that man doing down there?"

Max's head jerked up. Before he could comment, they both watched as the man leapt over the first ball, but tripped on the second, landing flat on his face at the end of the lane and knocking down all of her pins.

"Strike!" Max muttered only loud enough for her to hear.

She glared at him from over her shoulder.

The man staggered to his feet and Shayna shouted down the lane, apologizing profusely. Once again, Sunny appeared at her back. He patted her shoulder. "Don't worry, that happens, too." Then he made his way down the lane to help up the man who'd come down to change the lightbulb she'd broken.

Shayna spun around to face Max. "That's it. I'm getting out of here. You can finish the game if you want, but I'll be waiting for you outside."

Shayna went to the counter to exchange shoes and Max was right behind her. On their way out, he put his arm around her shoulders. "Don't worry about it, Shayna. That's probably the most excitement Sunny's seen in weeks. I'm sure you made his day."

When they reached his Pathfinder, Shayna turned to look at him. "You don't worry about anything, do you? Nothing fazes you. You're perpetually looking on the bright side and, as if by magic, things just always work out."

He took her chin in his hand. "Not always, Shayna, but a lot of the time. Worry is a self-fulfilling prophecy. If you're afraid things will go wrong, they will. You have to believe everything is going to be fine."

Then he dipped his head and very gently and briefly brushed his lips against hers. While she recovered from that unexpected kiss, he reached around her and unlocked the passenger door.

Shayna got in beside him, carefully thinking over his words. It was her nature to worry. That's why her business worked so well. She could foresee everything that could possibly go wrong and plan for it. While it worked in business, maybe it was the wrong approach for her personal life.

That area had not been running smoothly at all. For a while she'd been able to blame it on the chain letter, but now that was behind her and couldn't be the source of her problems. Her cheeks stung at the image of her mailing out those six letters. She'd really been desperate at that moment.

She'd spent all this time trying to change Max and

his life-style, but maybe he'd had the right idea all along. Well, his closet *had* needed some work, but maybe he'd been right about the rest. She was so uptight all the time, things just couldn't help going wrong.

She needed an attitude adjustment. She caught her tense reflection in the side view mirror of Max's Pathfinder. Shayna Gunther needed to lighten up.

As if on cue, Max turned up his favorite Motown station. An up-tempo song by the Commodores was playing. Another she'd always liked.

Max launched in wholeheartedly. He sang all the verses, and when the chorus came up, he tapped her knee, inviting her to join in.

Without thinking twice, Shayna did. And was rewarded with a bright toothy grin from Max.

He continued to sing and Shayna joined him, singing as loudly and off-key as he did. When the song was over, they both laughed until tears formed in Shayna's eyes.

A new song started and Max began singing. Shayna shook her head. "I don't know the words to this one."

Max shrugged. "Neither do I. Just fake it."

"What?"

"Make them up." Max listened to the music for a second, then chimed in with his own version. "Scooby-dooby doowah, I love you, that's no hoo-hah, a ratta-tat-tat…and you can't beat that with a bat!"

Shayna giggled uncontrollably, then she felt Max's

hand on her knee, indicating that she should take the next verse. "Um, a whop boppaloobop a bippity-boppity boo! Max is so crazy, he eats cereal from a shoe. A zippity doo dah, and a hi-dee hi-dee hay, they squish and a-squash when he runs every day!"

Laughing all the way home, they took turns rewriting lyrics to whatever songs came on the radio, even the ones they knew. When they finally pulled into Max's driveway, Shayna was out of breath. She couldn't remember the last time she'd acted so silly or had so much fun.

He turned off the engine. "Wait a minute. We never finished today's consultation."

Shayna shrugged. "Why don't we just forget it? You seem to do just fine on your own."

"Maybe, but you were right about my closet. It's much easier to pick out a pair of shoes in the morning when I know where both shoes are at a glance. And my dad stopped by the other day and was very impressed by the way we'd reorganized the kitchen. He thinks there may he hope for me yet."

"Good. I'm glad at least some of my ideas were helpful."

"Shayna, many of your ideas were helpful, and I think there's a lot more I could learn from you."

She'd already learned a lot from him, too.

"Besides, we haven't tackled the bathroom yet, and you haven't even *seen* my attic."

It filled her with pride to see Max so enthusiastic to continue their sessions. "Okay, if you're really interested, we can have a few more consultations."

"I am, but I do need to make one thing clear." He leaned forward. "I can't promise not to do this." His mouth closed over hers in a long, deep kiss.

"Mmm." Shayna gathered up her things and reached for the handle of the door. "Good. Perks are welcome in any job."

10

It was a beautiful afternoon for MBO's spring picnic. The sun sparked off the lake, which was surrounded by tall, willowy trees. MBO members played softball and Frisbee, and the smoky scent of hamburgers and barbecued chicken cooking on the grill filled the air.

Dressed in denim shorts and a red T-shirt, with her hair tied back in a ponytail, Shayna headed for the food tent.

"Shayna!" Lynette jogged up behind her and slung an arm around her shoulder. "What have you been up to lately, girl?"

"Nothing special."

"Well, whoever 'nothing special' is, I can't wait to meet him."

Shayna grinned at her friend. "I don't know what you're talking about."

"Come on, Shayna. You've got that look."

"What look?"

"Your eyes are sparkling, there's a spring in your step and you walk around grinning for no reason. And do you want to know what the most telling sign is? You helped them set up the picnic grounds without drawing the guys a detailed map of where everything should go. It's got to be love."

Shayna shrugged, slyly. "Healthy living and a satisfying career have the same effects."

Lynette shook her head. "Only a man would make you blush like that. You're not talking, huh? That's okay, I have a good idea who the lucky man is. Just make sure I get an invitation to the wedding." She glanced down at her watch. "It's time for my canoe ride with Ronald. I'll see you later."

"Bye." Shayna stared after her friend, not really seeing the view before her. Instead, she wondered if it really was that obvious. In these past couple weeks, she *had* felt a change come over her. She was beginning to see the world in a slightly different way.

It no longer seemed important that she fold the linens precisely in sixths or whether the toilet paper rolled out over or under. If she emptied her recycling bin on Thursday instead of Tuesday, no big deal. Maybe she *was* loosening up a bit.

In helping Max organize his life, she'd begun to learn a few things herself. As much as she scheduled her personal life down to the last detail, she hadn't been taking the time to try new things, to have fun just for the sake of having fun.

When she introduced Max to contact paper and handy wall-mounted storage racks, Max introduced her to in-line skating and all its perils.

Shayna taught Max to make hospital corners and use duvet covers, and Max taught her to blow up alien invaders in Battle Galaxy 2000.

After she took him to IKEA for cubbyholes and storage compartments, Max took her to Camden Yards for her first Orioles game.

They'd been having a good time, and she was feeling pretty happy, but love?

"Shauna! Hey, Shauna."

It took few seconds for Shayna to realize that the excited call from behind was meant for her. She turned and found none other than Phillip Browning, Jr. heading her way.

Dread filled her at the sight of him. The day was too beautiful to spend in captivity, and she had no interest in his various software creations.

"Shauna, how have you been?" he asked, stopping in front of her.

She didn't bother correcting her name; instead, she took advantage of what might be her only chance to speak.

"Oh, it's so nice to see you again. I've been keeping very busy lately. I pruned my lawn, regrouted my bathtub and even found the time to alphabetize my kitchen spices. It has been an exciting month."

"Actually, I've—"

"Oh, I'm sorry I have to rush off but—" she glanced down at her watch "—I'm late. It was nice talking with you, Patrick." She spun on her heel and continued her search for the food tent, wishing she could have seen Phil's expression.

She entered the tent, and the first thing that caught her eye was a basket of fresh strawberries. She grabbed a plate and began helping herself. Her hand collided with someone else's at the bottom of the basket.

She looked up and her gaze clashed with Frederick Montgomery's. He pulled his hand out of the basket as though he'd been burned and quickly backed away from the table.

Shayna shrugged. "So he doesn't like to share. Good. That leaves more for me," she said, loading her plate with the sweet red berries.

Leaving the tent, she searched for a quiet place to eat her fruit and enjoy the warm weather. She found the perfect spot at the top of a grassy hill, where she could watch the softball and Frisbee players.

Shayna nibbled on her berries, watched the players and daydreamed about Max. He'd said he would be a little late coming to the picnic because he had some errands to take care of. She secretly suspected that he'd wanted to sleep in. They'd been up late the night before at the craft fair. Shayna had insisted they spend some time hunting for bargains, and in exchange Max had demanded equal time at a computer show.

She was just about to reach for another strawberry, when a brown, masculine hand snaked over her shoulder and picked up a berry. "May I?"

Max! "Of course, you don't have to ask."

"That's very generous of you."

She looked over and nearly dumped her plate in the grass when she realized the man who had plopped himself down beside her was not Max Winston. It was Jason McKnight.

''Mmm. These are delicious.'' He reached out for another one.

She playfully swatted his hand away. ''Oh, no. If you want more, you'll have to find your own.''

Jason laughed. ''Oh, I see. You were generous until you realized I was a threat to your stash, huh?''

''That's right.''

''Okay, just point me in the right direction, and I'll be right back.'' He stood and dusted off his shorts. ''You don't mind if I join you, right?''

''Sure…uh, no problem.''

He jogged down the hill toward the food tent, and Shayna released the breath she'd been holding. Where was Max? What would he think if he came over and found her talking to Jason?

At that moment a hand clamped over her eyes. ''Guess who?''

Shayna reached up with both hands and tried to pry the hand away. ''Max, is that you?'' She wasn't taking any chances this time.

''None other.''

She continued to tug at his hand.

''Ah ah ah, not yet.'' He waited for her to relax and drop her hands; then he held a strawberry to her lips.

Shayna took a bite. ''Mmm.''

Max removed his hand and sat beside her. His eyes met hers as he bit into the strawberry he'd just offered her. ''Delicious. All we're missing is the chocolate fondue.''

She nodded. ''That would be perfect.''

He shrugged. "Since we don't have chocolate, I'll just have to be satisfied with a little sugar." He leaned in, angled his head and pressed his lips against hers.

When the kiss broke, she smiled up at him dreamily until she remembered that Jason would be headed back this way any minute.

"Those strawberries are good," Max said. "But I'm starving. I'm going to need something a little more substantial."

"There's all kinds of food in the tent at the bottom of the hill. Hamburgers, ribs, chicken, hot dogs…"

"Perfect. Do you want anything?"

"Maybe a hamburger?"

Max stood. "Let's see…medium-well, one leaf of lettuce, one tomato and lots of ketchup."

"Exactly, but maybe not as much ketchup as last time."

She could hear him laughing as he jogged down the hill. Seconds later, Jason's head appeared as he climbed the hill, carrying a huge plate piled high with strawberries and two cups of soda.

Shayna bit her lip, realizing that Jason and Max must have passed each other on the hill. They probably paused long enough to nod to each other before they continued on their way. What was she going to do with the two of them?

Jason set down his armload and stretched his long body out beside her. "I got you a soda. I hope you like orange."

"I do, thank you. But you didn't have to do that."

"It was my pleasure. I've been waiting for a chance for us to get to know each other better."

Great! She'd finally given up chasing after eligible bachelors and now they start chasing after her. It always worked out that way.

"What do you think about that?" He picked up a strawberry and bit into it suggestively.

"I've always said you can never have too many friends." She swallowed hard. Why did she feel so guilty? She and Max didn't have any kind of commitment, but she had the distinct feeling she was cheating on him.

Jason picked up another strawberry. "You should come down to the club some night—as my guest."

Shayna squirmed, watching the hill for Max. "I don't really have a lot of free time, and when I do, I don't go out much."

His grin widened. "Then we'll just have to change that. Do you like to dance?"

Her lips curved into a tiny smile as she remembered doing the salsa with Max in his bedroom. "Yes. I love it."

"Perfect. Then you'll love The Monument. Do you have plans tomorrow night?"

"I don't think so, but—"

"Great. Then it's a date. Most clubs have college night on Sunday, but The Monument is always twenty-five and over. We get a pretty sophisticated crowd. Perfect for a refined and lovely woman such as yourself."

"Jason, really, I didn't—"

"I have a confession to make. I might not have had the nerve to come over here and ask you out, if it weren't for one thing."

"What?" Yes, what? What had backed her into this cramped little corner?

"Lynette told me that you'd expressed interest in me. You and I have always been friendly, but I'd had no idea how you felt."

"Jason—"

"Don't get mad at her. She was just trying to help. Besides, it worked out because I feel the same way about you."

"I see." Not the most brilliant response, but it was the best she could do under the circumstances.

How could she tell him that she'd had that conversation with Lynette almost a year ago, soon after Jason joined MBO? How could she tell him her interest had moved elsewhere? How could she tell him she'd never agreed to a date with him?

But most importantly, how could she get him off this hill before Max found him there?

Shayna watched as Jason nibbled strawberries slowly. Unable to stand the mounting suspense, she wanted to grab the entire handful, shove them down his throat and send him on his way before Max returned.

Rejecting that idea, she decided to try something else. "You're not going to fill yourself up on strawberries, are you? They have an incredible spread down there. Hamburgers, fried chicken, potato salad, coleslaw…"

He stared at her lips. "You're making my mouth water."

"Well, then you'd better get some before it's gone."

"Can I bring you anything?"

"No, I'm fine."

"Okay, then I'll be back in a jiffy."

"On second thought, bring me a hamburger, please. Well-done. Very well-done, crispy—almost black. Richard probably isn't making them that way, so you'll probably have to wait for him to cook it. And put everything on it, pickles, onions, ketchup, mustard—everything. And I'll have some barbecued chicken, and—"

Jason laughed. "Why don't I just bring you one of everything?"

Shayna blinked at him, praying Max wouldn't appear over Jason's shoulder before she could get rid of him. "Okay."

He laughed again. "Shayna, you're a trip." He turned and loped down the hill.

She pressed her palm to her pounding heart in relief, then she spotted the extra plate and cup. Max would wonder where they had come from.

Moving quickly, she dumped Jason's remaining strawberries onto her plate and tucked his plate under hers. Then she poured his drink into the grass and stuck her cup inside it. She'd just set the cup and plate down beside her when Max's head appeared over the hill. How he'd managed to balance two loaded plates and two cups of soda on that steep incline, she'd never know.

He placed her plate in her lap and dropped down beside her. "Here you go. I took the liberty of giving you some potato salad and corn on the cob, too."

"Great. Thanks." She barely looked at her food, worrying that Jason would hurry back just as he'd threatened. "Why don't we go eat down there on those picnic tables? Come on."

He reached up and pulled her back down when she started to rise. "What are you talking about? We can't move. I just brought all this food up here."

She slumped back down and began to pick at her potato salad. "Okay."

"Hey," Max said suddenly, staring at the cup and plate beside her. "You already have a drink. I could have sworn you didn't when I left."

"Oh! Of course I did. You just didn't notice." Were beads of sweat collecting on her forehead? She wished her T-shirt had a collar so she could loosen it.

"You sure? Well, okay, never mind." He took a huge bite of his drumstick and loaded a fork with potato salad. "On the drive over here, I saw the most incredible…"

Shayna knew Max was still talking, but she couldn't get past the dull roar of panic that filled her ears. How was she going to avoid the awkwardness that would occur when Jason came back?

Just then she became aware of something cool seeping through her shorts. "Oh my goodness!" She leapt to her feet and stared at the spot where she'd been sitting.

"What is it? What's wrong?"

She continued to stare. She'd poured Jason's drink out on the grass behind her, like a dummy. Instead of sinking into the dirt, it had rolled down the hill. "I can't believe this."

Max stuck his hand into the wet spot. "Ugh! What is that?"

"I spilled my drink right before you came back."

He looked at the cup set off to one side. "But your cup is full."

She sighed. "I know. It was overflowing before. That's why it spilled."

"Oh. Well, here, let me help you clean up." He started handing her napkins and blotting at the grass where she'd been sitting.

"Uh, actually, I think I'd better clean up in the ladies' room."

This was the perfect opportunity for her to escape. She would go to the bathroom, Jason would come back, see Max, assume she'd left and then *he* would leave. She could straighten out the whole date misunderstanding with him later.

Max picked up his plate of food. "Okay, I'll wait for you here."

Shayna ran off in the direction of the bathroom, taking the long way around the side of the hill so as not to run into Jason on the way down.

Inside the tiny brown brick building, Shayna inspected each stall thoroughly before deciding it was safe. She hated park and recreation center lavatories because she'd always feared finding a snake or a raccoon lurking in the toilet bowl.

Shayna cleaned up as best she could, except for the huge wet spot on the back of her denim shorts. She repositioned her ponytail, checked her makeup and was preparing to leave, when Lynette walked into the bathroom.

"Lynette—just the person I wanted to talk to."

"Uh-oh," she said, circling Shayna and propping her hip up on the sink counter. "I don't know if I like that look in your eyes."

"Just tell me one thing. When and why did you tell Jason McKnight that I was interested in him?"

"Jason?" Her friend's face went blank for a moment. "Oh, that had to be at least three months ago, and I told him because I thought you never would."

Shayna frowned, biting her lip. "Three months? And he's just getting around to asking me out now?"

Lynette's eyes widened. "He's just now asking you out? I guess that means he's not the guy who put that sparkle in your eye. I guess it's better late than never."

Shayna sighed dismally. "No, in this case, never would have been better."

"What are you talking about?"

Quickly Shayna filled her in on the crazy game of musical men she'd been playing with Max and Jason.

"Oh, girlfriend, when you come out of the desert, you skip the stream and go straight for the ocean, don't you?"

"Yeah. Just keep your fingers crossed that this whole mess works out."

"You got it. Good luck, girl."

When Shayna got to the top of the hill, she was confronted with her worst nightmare.

Jason and Max were sitting together, engrossed in conversation. They both spotted her at the same time.

"Hey, Shayna," Jason said with open enthusiasm. "There you are."

"Yes, Shayna, there you are," Max said slowly, lacking Jason's enthusiasm. "Jason and I were just chatting. He was telling me about your *date* tomorrow night."

She wanted to melt into the ground at that precise moment. Max's eyes were hard and cold, though his expression was deceptively friendly.

"Yeah, I was just telling Max that he should come, too." Jason grinned at Max. "And bring a date. We can double."

"I don't think I'll be able to make it. I have other plans." Wadding up his napkins and tossing them onto his empty plate, Max stood. "Sorry to eat and run, but I've got to get going."

He didn't look at Shayna as he passed.

She looked at Jason grinning up at her and then at Max's retreating back. "We forgot to set the time for our next life management consultation. Excuse me."

As Shayna jogged down the hill after Max, she longed for her own life management consultant. Someone who could tell her how to handle this confrontation she was facing. Someone who might have been able to help her prevent it in the first place.

"Max," she shouted at his back. "Max, wait!"

He finally stopped halfway across the park grounds. He didn't turn, so she had to circle him to make eye contact.

"Let me explain what happened up there. It wasn't what it looked like."

His face took on a hardness she'd never seen before. "Of course, things are never the way they look, right? Jason told me quite clearly that he asked you to come down to his club tomorrow night, as his date."

"Yes, he did, but—"

"How did you think I felt when he showed up, carrying a huge plate of food that you asked him to bring you? If you wanted to spend the day with Jason, why didn't you just say so?"

"Max, please—"

"I foolishly thought you wanted to spend it with me, but I'm a grown man, Shayna. You don't have to play all these games. I've finally gotten the hint. I'm tired of chasing after you, when all you do is push me away."

"No! You don't understand. I didn't agree—"

"There you are, Max!" Ruth Warner, MBO's president, rushed over and grabbed Max by the arm. "I've been looking all over for you."

A petite, full-figured woman, Ruth had departed from her usual professional attire, opting for a pair of billowy red culottes and a matching vest over a white T-shirt.

"What is it, Ruth?"

She reached up to pat a few errant stands of her long hair, elegantly threaded with silver, into place. "We have an emergency. Our June speaker has conflicting engagements and has backed out of our program. I was hoping you'd fill in. Your file says you do workshops on—"

"I'll be glad to help out any way I can, Ruth. Just do me a favor and call me at home tomorrow. We can go over the details then."

"Thanks. I'll do that. You're such a dear." She squeezed Shayna's arm as she passed. "Have fun today, kids."

Shayna took a deep breath and tried to pick up where she'd left off. "I was trying to make you understand that I did *not* agree to go out with Jason. It was all a big misunderstanding."

"It always is." Clearly Max wasn't buying one word.

"Honestly. I'm not interested in—"

"Shayna, duck!"

"What?" She turned to look behind her and saw a red Frisbee headed straight for her head. She ducked just in time, and the Frisbee whizzed over in a gust of wind.

"Hey, are you all right?" One of the Frisbee players ran over and helped Shayna to her feet.

"I'm okay. I'm fine, thank you."

Max retrieved the man's Frisbee and handed it back, but the player lingered, still apologizing. "Are you sure you didn't get nicked?"

"Really, you missed me. No harm done."

Finally the Frisbee player wandered away, and Shayna turned back to Max. "Listen, this misunderstanding got started because Lynette told Jason that—" She paused when a friend of Max's came up behind him.

The man nudged Max in the ribs. "Have you tried this barbecued chicken?" He held his plate close to his face as he held the chicken leg to his mouth. "I'm telling you, it's the bomb!" he said with his mouth full.

His features still tight, Max turned to his friend and gave him a look that said "Not now!" "Yeah, I've tried it."

His friend remained oblivious. He took another bite, then noisily licked his fingers. "Mmm, mmm, gooood!" He glanced up and saw Shayna.

"Hey, I'm Tony. How are you?" He offered her a greasy hand.

Shayna just stared at his hand, unsure what to do without being rude.

Tony eventually got the message. "Oh, I'm bad." He wiped his hands on his shorts and extended his hand again.

Fortunately, Max chose that moment to intervene. "Look, Tony, Shayna and I were just having an important conversation, so if you don't mind..."

Tony's eyes widened. He looked back and forth between the two of them and then said, "Ooh, I'm sorry, man. I'll catch you later. You two just carry on."

Fearing another interruption, Shayna decided she'd better get straight to the point. "Max, please believe me when I say my feelings for you have not changed. I don't want to go out with Jason."

"Yeah, then why didn't you tell *him* that?"

"Like I said, there was a misunderstanding and everything got out of hand so quickly. I was confused."

He looked away and she knew he thought she was making excuses.

"Look, Lynette thought I was still interested in him, and she told him that, and I'm not, but she didn't know that because I was before." Realizing she wasn't making any sense, Shayna started again. "She didn't know I gave up my eligible bachelors list, and he waited a couple months to approach me, so the timing was all off. When he asked me out, he thought—"

"Wait a minute. What 'eligible bachelors list'?"

Shayna froze. Had she told him about that? Great, how could she explain? "It's no big deal really. Just a silly idea I had."

"A list of eligible bachelors...from MBO?"

She sighed. "Yeah."

"How long is the list?"

"Max, it really doesn't matter. I told you I've changed my mind about the whole thing—"

"Answer me, Shayna. How long is it?"

"Just three names."

"Is Jason on the list?"

Why was he grilling her like this? "Yes, but—"

"Am I on the list?"

Apparently her silence was all the answer he needed.

"That's what I thought."

"But, Max, none of that matters anymore."

"Yes it does. You've planned your life down to the last detail. You obviously know what you want in a man, and I'm not in your plan."

"Why won't you listen to me?"

"Because I should have seen this coming. I won't let you settle or pretend you want something you don't. Go out with Jason. You two probably have a lot in common."

"But I don't want to go out with Jason."

"I'm sure you will be very happy together. Go out with him. Enjoy yourself."

"Is that what you really want? You want me to see Jason?"

"Yeah, that's what I want. Maybe you can wreak a little havoc in his life for a change."

Shayna's body went cold. That was a low blow. Up until now, Max had never thrown her unfortunate quirks up to her. "Fine. If that's what you really want, then fine."

She spun on her heel and started stalking up the hill toward Jason. Halfway up, she stole a glance behind her and saw Max standing where she'd left him, watching her.

He was still watching her when she told Jason that she was looking forward to their date the next night. Max watched while she told Jason when and where to pick her up.

And Max was still watching when her heart broke into a million pieces.

11

What had he just done? Max asked himself, staring after Shayna. He'd spent months pursuing her, and he'd just blown it all in ten seconds of bad temper. At his insistence, Shayna was now at the top of the hill, confirming her date with Jason McKnight. Max felt like an idiot!

The next afternoon, he didn't feel any better. He couldn't get any work done because he kept glancing at the clock and wondering how many hours it would be until Shayna's date. It was the clock she'd made him hang above his computer so he could manage his time better. Instead, he was spending his time day-dreaming about her. He was tempted to call her up and beg her not to go, but he had the feeling she'd probably laugh in his ear and slam down the phone. It was no more than he deserved.

He'd tried to bury himself in his work, but he couldn't avoid the rotating desk organizer she'd gotten for him to de-clutter his desk, or the Stars of NBA Basketball calendar she'd sent him, or the countless little items that she'd scattered around his home to make his life easier.

He'd thought of himself as a good sport for going along with her life management ideas. His mind had been so focused on "fixing" Shayna, he hadn't even noticed that he'd needed some fixing himself.

Looking around, it was becoming apparent just how much he'd really needed her. The changes she'd made in his life had been so gradual. At first it had been as simple as moving a stick of furniture and buying a few office supplies. One clean closet here. An organized drawer there. Next thing he knew, his office was no longer the shadowy dungeon it had once been. He no longer tripped over shoes while getting dressed in the morning. It no longer took an eternity to put together a matching place setting at dinner.

Even if he could close his eyes to the things that were right in front of him, she was still there. Her image was a ghostly presence in his mind's eye. Her long dark hair. Her soft, slightly pouty lips. The graceful way she carried herself. The stunned, child-like expression her face took on whenever she broke, tripped over or spilled something.

The fact was, he was in love with her: determined, sexy, infuriating Shayna. He had no idea when it had happened, but it had been inevitable. Sometimes exasperating, often clumsy, always irresistible, Shayna was everything he wanted in a woman—and more.

He slapped his desk with his palm in resolution. He couldn't let her go out with Jason tonight. He looked up at the clock again. It was almost six o'clock. With any luck she hadn't left yet, and he'd still have time to catch her. Max reached for the phone.

No, he had to go see her in person, where she couldn't hang up on him, and she could see the sincerity in his eyes. He'd tell her how he felt about her and convince her to spend the evening with him instead.

Max rushed upstairs, grabbed his keys and raced out the door. He had to get to her before it was too late.

Shayna paced back and forth in her living room. She'd almost called Jason several times during the course of the day to cancel their date. She didn't want to go. Max was the only man on her mind.

Not only did the stubborn jerk not believe her, he wouldn't even listen to her. Still she dreaded spending an entire evening with Jason—not because he wasn't a nice guy, but because she no longer had any interest in him.

The doorbell rang and Shayna took one last deep breath. With any luck, the date would be horrible, and she'd have an excuse to go home early.

She tugged open the door, replacing her listless expression with one of forced enthusiasm. "Jason, it's good to see you."

He stepped inside dressed in a modern, well-tailored suit. His haircut was fresh. Shayna forced Max's description of her ideal man from her mind.

She had to admit. He looked handsome. His hands

were behind his back. He leaned forward and brushed his lips against her cheek.

"I'm pleased you agreed to spend the evening with me. I promise you won't regret it." He took his hands from behind his back and offered her a single yellow lily.

Shayna caught her breath. "Jason."

He smiled. "Roses are so overdone, and carnations are impersonal. We sat at the same table at the MBO banquet two years ago, and you admired the flower arrangement in the centerpiece."

Shayna tilted her head, stunned. "Are you telling me that you remember a comment I made at a banquet two years ago?"

He nodded. "I've always noticed you, Shayna. I was seeing someone else at that time, but I've always been aware of you."

She couldn't find words to respond. She took the flower into the kitchen to place it in water. Maybe Jason *was* Mr. Right, and she'd just let herself get temporarily forced off track by Max.

Her sister, Nicole, had gone through a phase in high school where she only dated guys who were all wrong for her. At the time, she was attracted to boys who rode motorcycles and smoked under the bleachers. Shayna hadn't gone through that phase, but maybe she was just a late bloomer. Maybe her attraction to a man who ignored clocks and feared schedules, who embraced disorder and was satisfied with clutter was her small rebellion against what she knew was good for her. Max was just a phase. And as she stepped onto the walkway beside Jason, she knew, it was time to grow out of it.

Max sat behind the wheel of his Pathfinder, watching as Jason McKnight led Shayna to his shiny black Lexus. Show-off.

He'd pulled up just in time to see McKnight walk up to the door with a lily behind his back. How pretentious. Max had circled the block, cursing himself for coming to his senses too late. A streak of masochism forced him to park nearby—not so close as to be seen, but close enough to watch them leave.

As their car passed him on the street, Max couldn't bring himself to go home. He pulled out of the parking lot, not really sure what he was going to do. All he knew was that Shayna had never given him the chance to take her out on a real date. He could be every bit as smooth and polished as McKnight.

During the ten minute highway drive, and for three city blocks, Max kept promising himself that at the next corner or stoplight he would turn around and go home. He wasn't going to follow Shayna on her date. That would be crazy.

Apparently love made people do crazy things because Max found himself following Shayna and McKnight into the restaurant portion of the nightclub. Afraid the hostess might seat him in full-view of the couple, Max requested a seat at the bar. He paid some teenager eating dinner with his parents twenty bucks for the use of his baseball cap.

The hat was too small, but Max was still able to

perch it on his head enough to pull the brim low over his eyes. McKnight and Shayna were seated a few tables to his right, so Max leaned his head into his hand and watched them through the gap in his fingers.

He couldn't hear what they were saying to each other, but he had a clear view of their table. Max watched with growing boredom as they perused the menu and made polite conversation. After they placed their order, Max became increasingly agitated. They seemed to be getting along.

He could hear Shayna's bright laughter as McKnight acted out whatever story he was telling her. Shayna raised a hand to her mouth, gazed at him through her lashes, then tossed her hair and appeared to giggle prettily.

Max's fists clenched at his sides. If he didn't know better, he'd say she was flirting with the guy! How dare she? And he hated what she was wearing. Why couldn't she have worn pants, or a conservative suit?

Instead she wore a gauzy V-neck blouse with long sheer sleeves that contrasted with her honey brown skin perfectly. She never wore sexy blouses like that when she was with him. In fact, lately she'd started coming over in jeans and T-shirts. Granted, the jeans were freshly pressed and creased and she always cuffed the sleeves of her T-shirts—because it looked neater, she'd said.

And where had she found that skirt? Sure the pink-and-white floral pattern might appear demure, but the hem stopped well above her knee. He'd watched her sashay into the restaurant. Between those strappy high-heeled sandals and that microscopic skirt, she made an alluring picture. He'd almost blown his cover and popped McKnight in the mouth for the appreciative look he'd given her as she walked in ahead of him.

He felt his anger rise again. How dare she go out with McKnight anyway? So what if he had insisted in a moment of temporary insanity. She still should have refused. Max and Shayna had really begun to build something. She'd gotten to the point that she no longer shied away when he kissed her. He'd known if he'd made the move, she would have let him finish what they'd started in his bedroom a few weeks ago.

Instead, he'd wanted to impress her with his patience and respect for her. He always halted their physical encounters before they could get that out of hand again. And they'd been having fun together. He could honestly say that she'd begun to loosen up. By that same token, some of her ideas had really made his life easier. Now he could actually find things on his desk and in his closets. They were good for each other.

How could she forget all that and go out with another man?

How could he have forgotten all that when he'd pushed her away? For a few minutes he'd let his ego rule his head. It had hurt that she hadn't felt he was worthy enough for her eligible bachelors list. Now, he knew she'd paid him an even bigger compliment: she'd gone against everything she'd thought she wanted in a relationship and had chosen him. Instead of cherishing that, he'd ruined everything.

Sucking in his breath, Max turned away and asked the bartender for another drink.

"Are you sure," the man asked. "This is your third one. I don't want to hear about you getting into trouble on the way home."

Max rolled his eyes at the man's sarcasm and took a long swig of his root beer. He needed to be alert.

The waitress finally brought McKnight and Shayna their meal, and Max waited patiently for Shayna to spill her water or drop her food in her lap. McKnight looked like another stuffed shirt, like that Frederick Montgomery. Once he realized how clumsy Shayna could be, he'd show his true colors.

With growing frustration, Max watched the couple eat half their meal and Shayna hadn't lost so much as a kernel of corn from her plate.

No way, Max thought to himself. He couldn't let Shayna continue this date without seeing McKnight as he really was. If Shayna wasn't going to cooperate, he'd just have to take matters into his own hands. It was for her own good.

Of course, it had nothing to do with his jealousy over seeing her with another guy.

Holding out a bill, Max flagged down a waiter.

"Yes, sir. How can I help you?"

"I was wondering if I could pay you for a little favor."

"What do you have in mind, sir?"

When Max explained what he needed, the young man blanched. "Sir, that's my boss. I'll be fired."

He handed the man another bill. "He's trying to impress the lady. I'm sure he won't fire you."

"But, sir, once the lady is gone…"

Max took out one more bill and his business card. "Okay, this is my final offer. If he fires you, give me a call. A friend of mine owns a restaurant in the city and the tips are incredible."

The man folded the bills into his breast pocket. "As you wish, sir." There was a gleam in the young waiter's eye as he carried a tray of desserts over to McKnight's table.

Max watched with anticipation as they each placed an order. As the waiter was about to leave, he pretended to trip and dumped the entire tray on McKnight's head. Max almost laughed out loud at the slice of chocolate cake nestled among the tight curls in McKnight's hair. Raspberry icing dripped onto his nose, glazed lady fingers sat on his shoulder, and when McKnight sprang to his feet, white frosted tiramisu slid down the front of his suit.

Max listened for the explosion, but whatever McKnight was saying, he didn't raise his voice. The young waiter hovered and fussed, and McKnight whispered something in his ear before the waiter rushed off to the kitchen.

Shayna handed him her napkin, but McKnight politely declined and hurried off in the direction of the men's room. It wasn't quite the reaction Max had been hoping for. In fact, McKnight probably scored a few more points with Shayna for remaining so calm. Max grit his teeth.

He looked over at Shayna sitting at the table alone. He had one last shot. He could run over to the table, throw her over his shoulder and kidnap her before McKnight returned. He wouldn't know where to find her, and Max wouldn't turn her loose until she forgave him and promised to stay away from any more eligible bachelors.

Max grinned at the image of Shayna over his shoulder. He'd carry her out to his truck and kiss her until she forgot her own name. Then he'd peel away that filmy little blouse and cup her honey-sweet—

He'd been so caught up in his fantasy that he hadn't realized that Shayna was staring in his direction. Oh, no, she'd seen him. His panic heightened when she stood and began walking toward him. Max froze. There was no way to—

Then he noticed that her gaze was directed beyond him. The ladies' room. Still, he couldn't risk her recognizing his face as she passed. Quickly, Max buried his face in his hands and pretended to sneeze uncontrollably.

"Bless you," he heard her say behind him.

"Thanks," he grunted, keeping his hands in place until he was certain she had gone.

When they both returned to their table, McKnight had removed his suit jacket and cleaned up. Shayna said something to him and they both laughed boisterously. Feeling dismal, Max wished he'd stayed home.

He watched as McKnight led Shayna to a set of

stairs at the back of the restaurant. The nightclub. Waiting a suitable amount of time, Max followed. If they saw him, he'd just say he decided to take McKnight up on his offer to stop by.

Max got to the bottom of the stairs and found himself facing a hulking bouncer. The man held up his hand to hold Max back. "Sorry, this is a private party. The club doesn't open until nine-thirty. Please come back then."

Max decided to give it one last shot. "Jason McKnight invited me personally. He'll be offended if you don't let me in."

"You must have misunderstood, sir. Come back at nine-thirty. Mr. McKnight left specific instructions. He wants to be alone with his date."

Max turned away and headed back up the stairs, his heart sinking into the soles of his Air Jordan tennis shoes.

Shayna squinted in the dark room, trying not to trip over anything as Jason led her through the dimly lit room. "There's no one else here, and why is it so—"

Jason flicked a switch on the wall and the room became illuminated in soft light. Reflections from the mirror ball danced like stars in the center of the dance floor.

"—dark," Shayna finished needlessly.

Jason guided her toward the dance floor. "You said that you like to dance and the club tends to get noisy and crowded at times. You seemed like the type of woman who would appreciate a more intimate atmosphere.''

He raised his hand and made some kind of signal. The room filled with a soft and lilting slow song.

"Wow," she murmured. "I'm impressed."

He grinned. "What's the use of owning a nightclub if you can't show your date a little special treatment?" He led her onto the dance floor and pulled her into his arms.

Shayna rested her head on his shoulder and tried to concentrate on Jason. Unfortunately, Max was interfering again. He'd been on her mind throughout the date, so much so, she'd even convinced herself that she'd seen him in the restaurant.

Jason had gone to so much trouble to make the date special, he deserved her full attention. He was everything she'd said she wanted in a man. He had a good job, always said the right thing, and had been a perfect gentleman even when that clumsy waiter had dropped the dessert tray on his head.

Shayna missed a beat, which Jason effortlessly compensated for. He did that a lot, whenever she dropped the ball, he'd swoop in and pick it up, as though they were in perfect sync. They did seem to think a lot alike.

They discovered over dinner that they had a lot in common. Jason clearly held the same affection for schedules and routines as she did. He'd had the timing of the date down to a science. The Monument was exactly twenty-two minutes from her house, they had drinks and small talk for fifteen minutes, dinner at precisely seven o'clock. To her surprise, she'd begun to think he was a bit rigid. At least they felt the same way about politics, religion, family values and work ethics.

In fact, Jason had given her a couple of tips on organizing her finances. Instead of making her excited, that had only annoyed her. She could manage her own finances just—

Oh, no! Is that how Max had been feeling all these weeks when she'd been trying to reorganize *his* life? Had she made him feel as though he couldn't manage his life on his own? She hadn't wanted to insult him, but now she had to admit that she probably had.

No wonder Max had been so anxious to get rid of her. She was finally beginning to realize how she'd been treating him. Yes, she *had* lightened up a lot in those last couple of weeks, and Max *did* seem receptive to many of her ideas, but that didn't make up for the heavy-handed approach she'd taken initially. Even if he never wanted to speak to her again, she owed him an apology for that.

Of course, he'd been pretty upset by her eligible bachelors list. And he'd had a right to be. It had been ridiculous for her to assume she could conduct her love life the way she conducted her business affairs. But, if he'd allowed her to explain, she would have told him that she'd changed her mind. She'd come to value his spontaneity, boyish sense of humor and hot kisses, more than punctuality and a healthy respect for order.

Shayna stopped dancing, suddenly realizing what her thoughts meant for her current date.

"Is something wrong?" Jason asked.

She picked up her step. He was her date, and regardless of her feelings for Max, she couldn't ignore him. "No. I was just thinking about how nice it was of you to give that waiter a break. Most men would have fired him for that kind of accident."

He laughed. "I couldn't fire him over something like that. I mean, it's not as though he did it deliberately."

"Well, I think it's still wonderful that you're so understanding. I know how he must have felt. Lately I've had my share of accidents."

"Really? That's hard to believe."

"Oh, no. Sometimes—" Shayna thought about what Jason had just said. It was hard for him to believe she had a clumsy streak because she'd been perfectly graceful the entire evening. She hadn't so much as broken a nail. It would seem the old Shayna was back.

Or was she? She did have her good days. Things usually went smoothly at work and even at home. In fact, the only time her clumsy streak kicked in was when she was around—

"Max!"

This time Jason stopped dancing. "What did you say?"

"Um…I don't know. I don't feel very well. I'm getting a headache. Would you mind taking me home?"

"Home? The evening's still young. I'll get you some aspirin—"

"No, I'd really better lie down. Please? Take me home."

Max was still sitting in the parking lot with his head resting against the wheel, trying not to imagine what was going on in the deserted nightclub Mc-Knight had taken Shayna to. That's why he was startled to see her emerge from the building after less than fifteen minutes.

They walked to McKnight's Lexus in silence. Max became instantly alert. What could have happened? He probably tried to make a move on her and Shayna had stalked out in a huff.

Max started his engine and pulled out a respectable distance behind them. If he hurt her, he'd break McKnight's neck.

Or maybe things had gotten so hot and heavy, McKnight was rushing her back to his apartment. Max pressed his foot down on the accelerator. If he touched her, he'd kill him.

Max stayed closer once they pulled into Shayna's complex. It was dark, so he wasn't worried about being seen. He parked where he could keep an eye on them.

McKnight walked her to her front door, and Max held his breath waiting to see if she would kiss him good-night. Max exhaled in relief when she gave him a quick hug and disappeared into the house.

He watched McKnight walk to his car—just to be

sure. He sat there a minute, trying to decide if he should knock on her door. No. He'd wait until morning. She might think he'd been hanging around her town house waiting for McKnight to leave.

He was just about to turn the ignition when he heard a tapping at his window. He looked up and saw Shayna standing at the passenger door.

He was busted.

Max stared at her for a moment and she motioned for him to unlock the door. He flicked the automatic door locks and she climbed in beside him.

"Park your car in that space over there," she said, directing him down the street, to the spot in front of her house. "We have to talk."

12

Max walked through Shayna's front door like a prisoner on death row. It was over.

"Have a seat," Shayna said, starting up the stairs. "I'll be right down. I'm just going to change into some sweats."

Max sat on her sofa stiffly. She wasn't even going to give him the pleasure of looking at her legs while she chastised him. He began to look around the room to take his mind off his building nervousness.

Her place was nothing like he'd expected. He'd envisioned pristine white furniture covered in plastic, tasteful artwork decorating the walls and elaborate floral arrangements on porcelain pedestals. Her home was far more down to earth than he'd imagined.

It was meticulously neat, but there were personal touches of Shayna everywhere. A collection of straw baskets dotted the room with anything from miniature teddy bears, silk flowers or the latest fashion magazines arranged inside. The paintings in the living room were watercolors and the walls of the front hall were decorated with picture frames that featured members of Shayna's family, including her adorable niece Tiffany.

Shayna came downstairs with her hair in a ponytail. He mentally nodded with approval. The white tank top she wore showed off the rounded lift of her breasts. Her navy blue sweat shorts gave him a pleasant view of her shapely legs all the way down to where her ankles disappeared into a pair of fuzzy bunny slippers.

"So you caught me," Max said when she stopped in front of him. "How did you know I was outside?"

"The last time we went out, I meant to mention that one of the bulbs in your fog lights burned out. I noticed you behind us on the highway, then I thought I saw your truck again in the parking lot. I went out the back door and sneaked up behind the truck, and, sure enough, it was you."

An embarrassed heat stung his cheeks. "I guess you'd like to know why I was following you."

Her expression didn't change. "Sure, I'd like to hear what you come up with."

Feeling ridiculous, he took a deep breath. She wasn't giving him an inch. "There really isn't a good explanation. Just the truth."

She stood waiting, brows raised and hands on hips.

"I really hated the way I let things get out of control at the picnic yesterday," he said, staring down at his hands. "I thought about you all day long. The thought of you and Jason together started getting to me."

He looked up to gauge her reaction. No change.

Her face wasn't telling him anything. "At some point, I got the crazy idea that I could come over here and talk you out of dating McKnight. Maybe even convince you to spend the evening with me instead."

He watched her face. She didn't speak, but her eyes seemed to soften.

"I came to my senses too late, though. I got here just in time to see McKnight pick you up." He squirmed on the sofa. There was no intelligent way to explain the rest.

"Go on," she prodded.

"I was planning to turn around and go home, but my truck had a mind of its own. I found myself following McKnight's Lexus to The Monument."

That's when Shayna backed up and sat on the chair across from him. "You followed me all night?"

"It wasn't planned. I was worried about you, but mostly it was torture. Seeing you laughing and having a good time with someone else was killing me. I spent the whole evening wishing you were with me."

She made an unintelligible sound, and Max knew she must have been shocked.

"I know. It doesn't even make sense to me, so I don't expect you to understand. All I can say for myself is that love makes a guy do crazy things."

Her eyes went wide. "Are you saying you're in love with me?"

Max felt his embarrassment double. "What other explanation could there be?" he answered, staring at her shag carpeting.

Suddenly, two bunny faces moved into his line of

vision. He looked up to find Shayna standing before him once again.

She looked into his eyes. "That's a pretty significant revelation. Tonight, I came to an important conclusion myself."

"What is it?"

Shayna knelt in front of him, placing her hands on his knees. "Never go out with one man, when you're in love with another."

His mouth instantly went dry. Had he heard her correctly or was it wishful thinking? "You're saying you're in love with me?"

She moved in closer so her lips were just inches from his. "What other explanation could there be?"

He closed the distance between them, letting his lips glide over hers. Groaning, he wrapped his arms around her and scooted forward to bring her into the space between his legs.

Her arms slid around his neck, and he deepened the kiss, releasing his tension. Her lips were a soft, open invitation, and he was ready to lose himself within her.

He pulled back to make sure she wasn't a very elaborate fantasy. Max inhaled her delicate perfume and stared into her honey-gold eyes. "When did you realize you love me? You and McKnight seemed to be getting along well. A little too well."

She took a manicured fingertip and traced over the stubble on his jaw. He'd been so wrapped up in Shayna, he had forgotten to shave that evening.

"We *were* getting along well. Jason was the perfect

gentleman. An ideal date. In fact, he was everything I thought I wanted in a man.''

Max's grip around her waist slackened. This wasn't what he'd been hoping to hear.

''There is only one thing wrong with him.''

''What's that?''

''He isn't you.''

''I thought I was everything you didn't want in a man.''

Her smile was sincere. ''Why wouldn't I want a man who is heartbreakingly sweet? Thoughtful. Funny. Not to mention incredibly sexy.''

Max smiled smugly.

''Don't get me wrong. You make me crazy. Your laid-back attitude is maddening and your knack for landing on your feet is exasperating. Do you know that my life is only crazy and chaotic around you? I haven't been this out of sorts since high school. This is what you do to me...but I wouldn't have it any other way. Max, you're nothing that I thought I wanted in a man, but everything that I need.''

Max found her lips again, his excitement mounting quickly. He stood, wanting to feel the full length of her body pressed against his. She made sweet sounds in her throat as he nuzzled her neck.

''I missed you, Shayna.'' He let his lips trail up to her ear. He sucked her lobe into his mouth. Then he whispered, ''I want to make love to you.''

She drew back and stared into his eyes. He felt as though his heart had stopped beating in his chest. She turned away, and taking his hand in hers, she quietly led him up the stairs.

Once she and Max were in her bedroom, those crazy, chaotic feelings began to kick in. She wanted this so badly, but it had also been a long time. It had to be special.

Max pulled her into his arms. "You look stunned. Are you sure this is what you want?"

Her heart was pounding erratically in her chest, but her voice was confident. "Yes. I'm sure."

Shayna lifted her face to meet Max's waiting kiss and bumped her head on his chin.

"Ouch!" Max groaned, rubbing his jaw.

"Ooh, I'm sorry." She pressed her lips to his injury, brushing his skin with a soft, wispy kiss.

He grinned down at her. "All better."

Their lips came together. His kiss was more urgent now, and she felt that urgency, too. She parted her lips, allowing his tongue to enter her mouth. Moaning, she quickly began to unbutton his shirt.

A button popped off and skittered to the floor. "Oops!" She drew back, pressing her fingers to her lips. "I'm sorry!"

He shook his head. "Forget it. I've got more at home just like it." He pulled the fabric apart, letting the remaining buttons pop off.

Dragging her fingers over his smooth muscled chest, she savored his impatient groans. Giving him pleasure filled her with a wicked rush of power. He certainly had the power to make her shudder.

Shayna's entire body felt alive and vibrant. When his breath touched her neck, her nipples tightened.

His fingers found the hard buds, rolling and kneading the tiny peaks. She arched against his hand, gripping him tightly.

Max had a beautiful body. She'd always admired the sculpted outline of his muscles in his clothing, but the unveiled version was even better. His skin was like dark velvet, and thoughts of chocolate fudge once again leapt to her mind.

Then Max whisked her tank top over her head, dipping his mouth to one breast, and her thoughts became incoherent. Sensation took over.

His hands were roaming over her body as his teeth and tongue teased her satin-covered nipples. Her eyes drifted shut, and she searched blindly with her fingertips for his chest. She felt smooth skin softer than silk. Her fingers found crisp curling hairs trailing down the center of his chest. Following the trail, her palms discovered hard muscles, unyielding like steel.

Suddenly it seemed too much. She wanted to see him. All of him. Her eyes flew open and her heavy-lidded gaze instantly collided with Max's. His eyes were filled with such tenderness and love, she felt her knees weaken.

Lifting her effortlessly so her feet no longer touched the ground, Max sat on the foot of her queen-size bed, bringing her down on his lap.

She watched his lips part as he sucked in an excited breath. He reached around her back, and with trembling fingers, unhooked her bra. Max slid it off her body, quickly cupping the fullness of her breasts.

Shayna's eyes fluttered closed again as she absorbed the sweet pleasure of his touch. His hands massaged and caressed from her neck to her waist. She bucked on his lap, feeling his arousal through his jeans.

Groaning, Max fell backward onto the bed and Shayna tumbled forward, sprawling on his bare chest. Then they were sliding and...falling. The comforter slipped off the bed, and they slipped with it. Max, who landed on the bottom, shielded her body from the impact. Shayna started to move off him, but Max held her in place.

"It's probably safer if we stay right here." He reached behind her and yanked the comforter completely from the bed.

She leaned forward, pressing her mouth over his. They kissed hotly, their lips moving frantically, trying to deepen their kisses as much as possible.

Max rolled her onto her back, leaning back on his heels as he began tugging at the waistband of her shorts. He brought them down her thighs and over her ankles.

Not wanting to let him get too far ahead, Shayna sat up and reached for his waistband. She unfastened his jeans and stripped them off.

He came down on top of her, kissing and nuzzling her neck as Shayna cupped his buttocks in her hands. She fondled and massaged the firm muscles, causing Max to moan and grind against her.

"I can't wait much longer, Shayna."

"Wait," she whispered. She reached into her night table drawer and pulled out a fabric-covered box. Pressing a small package into his hand, she said, "You know my motto is to always be prepared."

He kissed her tenderly as he stripped away the final barriers between them. Shayna arched against him, loving the contrast of his hard muscled body against her softer one.

Max gently spread her legs and slowly entered her. Shayna felt an uncomfortable tightness, but pleasure quickly began to grow as he lowered himself into her.

Together they began to move, their bodies rocking and grinding as their excitement mounted. Max whispered in her ear, and Shayna gripped his arms tightly.

"Baby, you feel so good," he said.

Sensation began to build. "Oh, Max!"

Realizing her pleasure was about to peak, Max moved more quickly above her. Their bodies came together faster and faster.

Finally, she heard Max moan her name in her ear, and Shayna was not far behind him. Suddenly her body went weak as a jolt of release vibrated through her.

Max withdrew and collapsed beside her. He gathered her against him. "I waited so long for you, Shayna, and it was more than I could have hoped for."

Sleepily, she rested her head against his chest. "Perfect. I love you, Max."

* * *

When Shayna's eyes popped open the next morning, she saw a dark muscular arm draped over her waist. Curling against him, she relived last night in her mind.

Making love with Max had been wonderful…if a little awkward at first. She loved him for all his quirks and habits, and he loved her. Despite her occasional accidents and her compulsive tendencies.

It wasn't bad luck or chain letters that caused her flustered, embarrassing moments around Max. It was Max. Or rather, his unusual effect on her. Even though he didn't seem to have a problem with this strange side effect of her feelings for him, she couldn't imagine making him suffer through a relationship with her burning, tripping and spilling whenever they were together.

Things were going to have to change.

Shayna was so engrossed in her thoughts, she didn't notice that Max had awakened. Suddenly the arm slung across her waist began to make small gentle circles over her hip.

Rolling onto her side, she looked into his eyes. His sleepy expression was happy and satisfied. ''Morning,'' he whispered.

''Good morning, Max.'' If she were going to establish a change in their relationship, now was the time.

''I've been thinking…'' she said, and he leaned forward and began nibbling on her neck.

Max scooped her up and rolled her on top of him. ''I've been thinking, too, about this, in my dreams.''

She braced her hands on his chest and looked down at him. "Now that we've admitted how we feel about each other, don't you think we should discuss…things?"

His hands smoothed up her back. "What kinds of *things*," he asked wickedly.

Shayna rolled off of him. His caressing fingers, not to mention his naked body beneath her, made it impossible for her mind to function properly.

"Our future." She stared up at the ceiling, sorting her thoughts. "Let's see. We've been dating *in*formally for a while, so it stands to reason that we'll have to date *formally* for…what do you think? Six months?"

Max propped himself up on his elbow. "What did you say?"

Shayna continued, wrapped up in her plans. "After six months we can begin to discuss wedding plans." She rubbed her chin. "Is that soon enough?"

Just to make sure, Shayna opened a drawer in the night stand and pulled out a list written on pink stationery. She crossed off the first two items with a pen and carefully contemplated what followed.

"Yes, that way I can still be married before my thirtieth birthday. I think it's nice to be married for at least two years before having children, don't you?" She looked up at Max, who was staring at her, clearly dumbfounded. "Max?"

Shaking his head he got up from the bed and tugged on his boxer shorts. "I thought you were joking, but apparently you're still trying to plan out every last detail of our lives."

Shayna pulled on her bathrobe and crawled across the bed. "Max, what's wrong? Those were just options. I don't *have* to be married before I turn thirty. How about thirty-one?"

He stopped dressing and looked pointedly at the list she held.

"I can be flexible." She quickly tore it in half and threw it over her shoulder. "See?"

Max shook his head. "I'm not buying it. I'll admit, you sold me on the values of organization. My life is running a heck of a lot smoother now that you've given it structure, but that doesn't mean I want to live a militant life-style. Fall in love at 0800 hours. Get married at 0900 hours. Have babies—"

"I get the idea." Shayna held up her hand to stop him, sinking backward onto the bed. "I guess I panicked a little. I'm sorry. I can't promise that I'm not going to be compulsive every so often. But I've changed…really. What can I do to prove that to you?"

Max rubbed his chin as he looked around her neat and orderly room. "Let's do a little experiment. If you and I are going to be together, we're going to have to compromise."

Shayna nodded. "I can handle that."

His grin was sly. "Oh, really?" He walked over to her dresser. "Then you won't completely lose it if I forget to close a few drawers sometimes." He pulled open all the drawers, then closed only half of them, making sure a bra strap, a T-shirt sleeve and a sock peeked out.

She took a deep calming breath. "I can handle that."

Max nodded, opening her closet doors. "Great. Then you won't mind if sometimes your clothes aren't in perfect order by color?" He began rearranging her hangers, mixing shirts with pants, dresses with skirts. He put blues next to yellows and greens with reds.

Shayna stared wide-eyed at her once perfectly ordered closet with her hands clamped tightly in her lap. "I can...handle it." She began taking shallow breaths.

Max raised a brow, clearly impressed. "Okay, here's the final test." He walked into her bathroom. She jumped to her feet and followed him.

"I'm a man, so I don't always remember to put the toilet seat down." He raised both lids, exposing the toilet bowl. Shayna bit her lip.

"I don't always refold towels after I use them. I like to put them back on the rack, open to the air. They dry faster that way." Max unfolded one of the towels in her shelving unit and spread it out on the towel rack. Shayna braced her back against the door frame. Were her knees getting weak?

"And if we were to live together, my things would take up half the space on this countertop." He began picking up her perfumes, nail polish, powders and lotions and rearranged them so they were all crammed on one side of the sink. He opened her medicine cabinet and changed the order of everything on the shelves. Then, just for good measure, he took her toilet paper off the roll and turned it the opposite way. "Well, what do you think?"

"I can—" Shayna blinked at the bathroom before her. Raking her fingers through her hair, she patted her forehead for beads of perspiration. She licked her lips and swallowed hard. "—handle it."

Max's lips quivered then he released a long laugh. He gripped her around the waist and pulled her into a tight hug. "I'm sorry, honey. I know that was torture for you. But you passed. Don't worry, I'll help you clean up."

Shayna hugged him back. "I do love you, Max. More than I love having things my way."

He picked her up and started carrying her toward the bedroom. "I love you, too, sweetheart."

She gripped his shoulders tightly. "Now, can I ask you something?"

He set her on her feet and backed up to look into her eyes. "What is it?"

"You said I sold you on the value of organization. Did you mean it?"

"Of course I meant it." He smiled tenderly, reaching out to stroke her cheek. "I know at first I acted as if I was merely humoring you, but that was only because I didn't want to admit that my life could benefit from a few changes. After I gave up the whole corporate routine, I was locked into that 'been there, done that' philosophy."

Shayna nodded slowly. "I know I've spent the past

few months force-feeding you my life management plan.''

''That's right. Together we nipped, tucked, folded and pressed my life into shape. And now that we have, Shayna, I wouldn't have it any other way. You're very good at what you do. That's one of the reasons why I love you.''

''I'm so glad to hear you say that.'' She grinned, dragging him over to the open dresser drawers.

''Now that we've established that, I won't lose my mind every time you leave something out of place. Let me also point out that I'm going to be too busy kicking back and enjoying life to clean up after you.''

After Max had restored her drawers to order, she pointed him toward the bathroom. ''Get to work, buddy.''

Max straightened up his mess under Shayna's careful supervision. ''There. Now the earth is back in alignment and all is right with the universe,'' he said, dusting off his hands.

''Not so fast,'' Shayna said wickedly. ''I'm not through with you yet.''

''Really?'' Max was clearly intrigued. ''Just what do you have in mind?''

''A little revenge.'' She began leading him down the stairs. ''Have you ever made love in the kitchen?''

''Uh…no.''

''Because I have this ongoing fantasy that involves you covered with chocolate. I'm warning you now, it's going to be a bit messy.'' She turned to look at his stunned expression. ''But don't worry,'' she said with a seductive wink. ''I'll help you clean up.''

13

"Max! Max, where are you?" Shayna leaned on the doorbell again. "I see your truck out front. I know you're in there."

He was supposed to have met her, Tiffany and Kenny at the park over an hour ago for the MBO Fourth of July barbecue. Finally she'd had to leave the kids with Lynette and drive over to find out what was keeping him. He'd never been overly concerned with punctuality, but this was ridiculous.

Suddenly the door jerked open and Shayna almost fell over the threshold. "Max, where have you—" She took in the huge wet stain on the front of his T-shirt. "What happened?"

Max frowned at her. "What hasn't happened? I spilled an entire pitcher of lemonade, I burned the baked beans I was bringing to the picnic—"

Shayna pinched her nose. "Oh, so that's what I smell."

"And my truck won't start. I've been waiting for emergency road service for over an hour."

Shayna grinned. It was amusing to see Max out of sorts for a change. Fortunately, her clumsy mishaps had been few and far between lately, but for the past couple of days Max had had one incident after another. Shayna was glad she hadn't cornered the market on bad luck.

"Call and tell them to come later. I'll give you a lift to the barbecue. Just change. And don't worry about the beans—we have plenty of food."

"Okay." Max ran upstairs to get ready, and Shayna went downstairs to watch television while she waited.

Sinking into his big leather chair, she couldn't help noticing a crumpled piece of paper sitting on top of his brand-new In bin. "This looks very familiar," she said, picking it up. "A chain letter!" Shayna laughed out loud.

"What are you laughing at?" Max entered the room, wearing a clean shirt.

Shayna waved the chain letter in front of her. "This."

He snatched it away from her, clearly embarrassed. "That's nothing. Just some silly letter Kenny sent me. I was going to throw it away."

She grinned, taking it back. "Oh, then let me help you." She balled it up and tossed it over her shoulder.

"Wait!" Max lurched forward, tripping over his feet and falling on top of Shayna, bringing them both down.

Shayna rolled him onto his back, cupping his face between her hands. "Don't worry, Max. I'm the only good-luck charm you need." Their lips came together in a soft open kiss.

"I agree, sweetheart. Spending the next fifty years with you is one plan I intend to stick with." He stared up into her eyes and then back at the crumpled paper now lying next to his head. "But maybe you'd better grab that letter...*just* in case."

* * * * *

Silhouette

SPECIAL EDITION ™ ®

In March 1999 watch for a brand-new
book in the beloved MacGregor series:

THE PERFECT NEIGHBOR
(SSE#1232)

by

1 *New York Times* bestselling author

NORA ROBERTS

Brooding loner Preston McQuinn wants nothing more
to do with love, until his vivacious neighbor, Cybil
Campbell, barges into his secluded life—and his heart.

**Also, watch for the MacGregor stories
where it all began in the exciting 2-in-1 edition!**

Coming in April 1999:

THE MACGREGORS: Daniel—Ian

Available at your favorite retail outlet,
only from

Silhouette ®

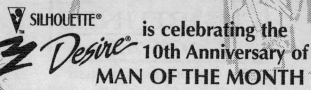
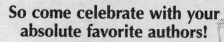

FORTUNE'S Children™

**The Fortune family requests
the honor of your presence at the weddings of**

Silhouette Desire's scintillating new miniseries,
featuring the beloved Fortune family
and five of your favorite authors.

The Honor Bound Groom—**January 1999**
by Jennifer Greene (SD #1190)

Society Bride—**February 1999**
by Elizabeth Bevarly (SD #1196)

And look for more **FORTUNE'S CHILDREN:
THE BRIDES** installments by Leanne Banks,
Susan Crosby and Merline Lovelace,
coming in spring 1999.

Available at your favorite retail outlet.

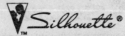

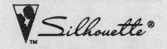

*Sneak Previews of March titles
from Yours Truly™:*

A MATCH FOR MORGAN
The Cutlers of the Shady Lady Ranch
by Marie Ferrarella

Morgan Cutler had thought her lifelong desire for
Wyatt McCall was long gone—until she discovered
he was single again. Troubled by the feelings he aroused in
her, Morgan struggled to keep him out of her thoughts.
But, with love and marriage in the air at the Shady Lady
Ranch, she secretly hoped it was only a matter of time
before this girl-next-door became his bride-to-be.

DID YOU SAY *BABY?!*
by Lynn Miller

When beautiful Rebecca Chandler showed up on his
Texas ranch, JD McCoy's calm life was suddenly
turned upside down. In her hands was his runaway sister's
baby…that *he* was supposed to take care of? Taking
pity on his lack of fatherhood know-how, Rebecca
stuck around to help the sexy stranger get used to his new-
found role. But when the mother surprisingly reappeared,
Rebecca's decision to leave made JD
realize just how much he felt for this woman—
and what he would do to hold on to her.